Based on true events

by

A.P.

Aristeiguieta

tito

PEACE OF HEAVEN

TITO
PEACE OF HEAVEN

TRIGGER WARNING:

The contenct of this book tackles sensitive topics such as depression, suicide and drug abuse. Reader discretion is advised.

This is a work of nonfiction. Nonetheless, some names, idetifying details and personal characteristics of the individuals involved have been changes. In addition certain people who appear in these pages are composites of a number of individuals and their experiences.

ACKNOWLEDGEMENTS

Thank you to all of those who think I'm crazy for believing in the possibility of other dimensions, extraterrestrial connections, lucid dreams; thank you for believing in my madness, because thanks to the fact that I was in denial at first, I was able to connect with certainly the most amazing dream I have ever had, that led me to a spiritual growth after being dead inside while my body was still alive.

My family, my parents, my brother and my sister in law, my dreams, Tito, his family, and last but not least, the universe for allowing me to put this book in your hands, a story full of doubts turned into truths.

Thanks in advance, to all of you reading this book.

Thank you to all of those who have believed in me and work with me to tell this story, to leave a message. I would have never made it on my own, life is all about collaborations.

TABLE OF CONTENT

SPOTIFY PLAYLIST

- Why me by Thiago Muller
- Perfect by Simple Plan
- Welcome to my life by Simple Plan
- Zapatillas by El Canto Del Loco
- Personas by El Canto Del Loco
- Todo lo hago mal by El Canto Del Loco
- Peter Pan by El Canto Del Loco
- Apologize by One Republic
- I kissed a girl by Katy Perry
- Say by John Mayer
- Let it go by James Bay
- Nothing Else Matters by Metallica
- Dream on by Aerosmith
- I don't want to miss a thing by Aerosmith
- Crazy by Aerosmith
- Caminando por la vida by Melendi
- De repente desperté by Melendi
- Just the way you are by Bruno Mars
- Wake me up by Avicii
- Hey soul sister by Train
- Misery Business by Paramore (Acustic)
- Wake me up when september ends by Green Day
- Hold on by Jonas Brothers
- Who I am by Nick Jonas
- Aunque no te pueda ver by Alex Ubago
- El problema by Ricardo Arjona
- Color esperanza by Diego Torres
- Puedes contar conmigo by La Oreja De Van Gogh
- Go the distance by Roger Bart (Hercules)
- You'll be in my heart by Phil Collins
- Reflection by Lea Salonga (Mulan)
- Hakuna Matata by Nathan Lane (Lion King)
- Girl on fire by Alicia Keys
- Because of you by Kelly Clarkson

PROLOGUE

I have always loved a good story and I truly believe in my heart that the greatest stories are the ones that have never been told. That is one of the many reasons why I fell in love with this specific story. I first learned about it when Andreina asked to see me and told me about a project she had been working on since 2016 and that her idea was to release it not only in a book format but also as a featured film. After reading the script's first draft and the book, I automatically fell in love with the story and Andreina asked me to be part of her journey as a producer in the movie. Of course I said yes without hesitation.

Two of the things that captivated me the most were Amy and Alberto's friendship and the way Amy's dreams are told. Let's start with the dreams. I am and have always been a firm believer that dreams are portals that take us to alternate realities to show us our deepest desires and also our greatest fears.

Dreams also introduce us to strangers, people we have never met before and all of a sudden we are walking down the street and there they are, the strangers in our dreams and we can't seem to understand how could we have dreamt about someone we have never seen before and out of the blue they are right in front of us when we least expect it. Maybe, just maybe life is sending them our way because they have been connected with us not just in this lifetime, but also in every other lifetime.

Now, let's talk about Amy and Alberto for a second. As you go through the book you will be as amazed as I was with their relationship since it is the kind of friendship that I personally have always wished to have and I can proudly say I have been lucky and blessed enough to find it. It is the kind of relationship that, as you are reading page after page, makes you dream while you awake.

Not long ago, I found out that this was the writer's personal story, that Amy is really Andreina Perez and honestly, it made me respect her even more. All I can say is that I am proud of her and all her accomplishments and for being strong enough to share her story with the world.

Alejandro Sequera

INTRO

Finally, you're here, getting to know me through my writing, my storytelling, my passion, my mission.

I spent many years thinking about whether I should do this or not, raising my voice, sending a message, but I never knew how to; I wasn't confident of its power, or even if it was worth taking the risk and putting myself out there to confirm what many of you might think already. I'm crazy as fuck!… and as you read through this, you will understand why.

Ever since I was little I believed in things that adults thought were "absurd", or "unreal", basically nonexistent. I'm pretty sure they still do. They would talk about me as someone who "fantasized" too much… Starting by the fact that I had a yard full of dinosaurs under my bed, whom I considered my friends. And to satisfy the thirst of "animal friends" or "imaginary friends" my mom got me an Agaporni, it's a kind of bird; I named him Esteban, he was my best friend until the housemaid crushed him with the sofa (accidentally, of course).

On one hand, I'm the one to blame, because he would run and fly free all over the house, but as a 'bird-pet' he is supposed to be caged (even though they belong to the sky, clouds and flying free through nature), mine wasn't: Esteban was free to come and go around the house as he pleased (under what was my concept of freedom), running all over the place, just like a puppy would.

After that, I was sent to a psychologist, because I accidentally told my kinder friends about the real dinosaurs under my bed; so my teacher suggested to my parents that I should be taken to see a children's therapist , and so I went. It was then, when I heard the words that would change my life forever: "What will people think?"

What you are about to read has nothing to do with what I just said; this is just an opening, so you can get an idea of what kind of person I am. None of these qualities define my kindness or the lack of it, it's just a little teaser of my personal beliefs.

I believe in things that are beyond what meets the eye, even more than the things that are in front of me.

What do you believe in?

Answer the questions below:

1. Do you believe in second chances? ________
2. Do you believe in miracles? ________
3. Do you believe in real friendship between women and men? ________
4. Do you believe in yourself? ________

This is the story of an ordinary girl with no extraordinary abilities, on the contrary, she was quiet and lonely, her outfits were colorful to its maximum that the only thing that would stand out was the misery within the reflection in her eyes; only visible to those brave enough to see through her beyond what the eyes could reach.

This ordinary girl without any ability is me: AMY.

CHAPTER 1

WHY?

"The acceptance of death gives you a wider and more creative vision of what life is; believe it or not, this understanding leads you to find your inner peace. You get answers from questions you didn't even know you had and from there, beautiful things come along."

MAY 17tH, 2008

I woke up at the hospital, lights were off… and like always, I was all by myself. I asked the universe to surprise me and to explain to me why I was here, and of course… where exactly?

I got out of my hospital room with the IV equipment attached to my arm. I kept walking and right at the end of the hallway I saw a shining child's silhouette. I knew it was a little boy, but I couldn't really see his face. He would keep jumping from side to side and waving at me as if he wanted me to follow him…

— Come — he said, even though I couldn't understand him, I knew what he wanted to say (I think he was around three years old or younger but definitely not older than that).
— Wait, who are you? Where are you going? — I asked. I kept walking faster and faster but he was bold at its maximum.

A light illuminated his silhouette; he ran slowly, like a baby does and walked towards an extremely bright white light that immediately blinded my eyes. And suddenly I found myself at home, I was walking through my house and the baby was guiding me through a specific path as if he knew me from another lifetime: we walked through the kitchen, he grabbed my hand and he pulled me with all his strength. Honestly he was like this magical kid you can't describe with words, his childish laughs and his eyes made me smile, he was kind and full of tenderness.

He then took me through the living room and the elevator opened; I pulled him so we could hide, but it wasn't really necessary. I understood that I was living a dream, I saw myself getting home and I somehow remembered this path. We began to follow my other self, and walked throughout the whole apartment; I remembered everything, or almost everything; I turned and looked at the calendar hanging in my room. It was like a deja vu.

SELF LOVE = ABSENT.

I asked myself, what am I? Instead of, Who am I? I stopped considering myself a human being the day I stopped caring, the day I began to walk through life careless, I was just a breathing, existing and my heart would beat just because it's his main function to keep us "alive", no wonder why it is the most important organ in the human body, because we could not live without it, or at least that's how I programmed my heart, o not feel or care about the things that were emotionally affecting me.

I was having problems at home: my mom would drown her emotions in alcohol while my dad would spend the whole day at the office, working to "please" us with everything we asked for, without understanding that material things would not fill the whole my mom felt every time he exited the door. He would always come back home late, way later than the actual office hours. My brother Derek, my favorite person in the whole world ignored my very existence, making me feel like I didn't matter, which lead me to concluded that I was: meaningless; we are told that siblings are supposed to have each others back, support and understand one another, but in my case I could only feel how I meant nothing to him, how his friends were more important than me, and I don't blame him, it was his way of escaping our parents divorce.

I tried telling myself that it was just a phase, a part of his life in which friends are more entertaining than his family… but we were going through the same phase: high-school, a dysfunctional family that would fight all day long for everything and anything.

My mom relied on her friends and alcohol, my father had his job and I'm pretty sure he also had another woman keeping him company; and my brother had parties, friends and a car he drove to run away from home when things would get ugly at home… As for me, I had a boyfriend, or so I liked to call him, but now that I look back we were anything but a couple, but we were 'something' as long as we were not seen together in front of his friends.

Honestly I didn't find any sense nor motivation whatsoever: I had no friends, I was a complete loner, and being with myself wasn't pleasant at all. I would go to school and my classmates would constantly bully me because of my looks, my lack of boobs or ass: not that my outfits helped or anything to be honest, so my chances of looking "pretty" were nonexistent, I would walk through the hallways with my headphones on to avoid listening to any type of insults or despicable comments.

I was once asked which super power I'd like to have, my inner voice didn't have to think twice: invisibility.

But before I continue, let's go back to what happened before my visit to the hospital.

BEFORE I WAS BORN AGAIN

MAY 16TH, 2008

I got home after a long regular day of school, nothing to tell… as usual. I entered my house and it was empty. I walked into my parents room and there was nobody there; I didn't even bother checking my brother's, I'm pretty sure he was with his friends. My house, like always, felt like a dark place in which I was nothing more than a grey spot nobody would notice, neither absent nor present.

Somehow I was still hopeful that something was going to light up my day, but I still walked through the house like a zombie, useless: I saw nothing but solitude in every corner. And so I decided to call my "boyfriend", Frank; and as if I didn't feel lonely enough, he didn't pick up, which added some spice to the cake. I sat on my bedroom floor and started to think and overthink my existence. The conclusion I came up with was poisonous to my head: *I meant nothing to the world, I had no purpose, no goals, no impact on anyone's life.* Why am I alive?: Since there is no answer to that, I guess sleeping was the only solution to end with another crappy day just to wake up the next day, hopeless knowing that my day will be as bad as it was today, if not worse.

Whatever, let's keep walking through life with no purpose, I'm used to it already, so I went to sleep, with no regrets.

`MAY 17tH, 2008 (AGAIN)

When I woke up, I couldn't see anything. I remember standing up and everything was moving, I was completely unbalanced and the road to the bathroom seemed so long. I finally got to the toilet and from one second to the next everything started to fade, even the sound of the morning birds singing was vanishing little by little. My surroundings changed to a misty and foggy white space, a mix between how I imagined 'heaven' and infinite.

I was only able to listen to a faded flat line coming from a heartbeat machine, someone was dying, death was near, I felt it inside me… All of a sudden, I could hear a soft voice which I couldn't quite understand until the flat line's sound suddenly stopped. Now I could only listen to that voice: *"baby, we are here with you, my love. We are waiting for you and we love you so much, please wake up"*; at that moment I could hear a soft heart beat sound on top of that sweet voice.

I began to open my eyes, slowly and involuntarily, and even though everything was a little hazy to me, I was able to distinguish the voice coming out of a speaker that was placed on a table next to a bed in which a baby boy was lying on, attached to tubes and machines, next to the bed I was in, and I couldn't remember why or how I ended up here.

Clearly I was having doubts, whether this was a dream or real life, or if what I thought was a dream was actually real. A young lady was sitting next to the boy who was next to me. She was holding his hand; I knew I've seen her somewhere before but I couldn't remember where, she looked so familiar. I turned my back on them and I saw my parents in the distance, arguing as always; as soon as they realized I was awake they walked towards me.

— Where did you get the drugs from, Amy? — My dad

asked.

— Who gave them to you? — My mom asked.

So many questions I was overwhelmed

— Wow, wait… what are you talking about? What am I doing here? — I answered, sweating, hyperventilating and confused.

— There is no need to lie, Amy. Your blood work came positive on drug overdose— my mom said.

— I don't remember, I think I just had a little bit too much alcohol, but I surely didn't do drugs — I told them.

— And where did you get the alcohol from? — my dad asked, overlooking my mom.

— The pantry — I said.

— Look at that, Angela, the pantry — my father said, with disappointment. I decided to turn around, I didn't want to be the reason of their next fight.

— So now you are blaming me, Jaime? — I heard my mom, full of anger.

I closed my eyes pretending to fall asleep to not hear anything until I actually fell asleep.

"YOU KNOW YOU HAVE A BIG HEART THE
MOMENT YOU FEEL GUILTY
FOR DOING WHAT'S BEST FOR YOU"

MAY 20tH, 2008 (2:00 AM)

I woke up again in that white foggy and empty space that I would like to call from now on: "safe haven", and there he was again, the baby boy from my dreams. He held my hand to walk me through, he was getting used to this and I couldn't understand why, but I liked it. This time he took me to the hospital waiting room where we were both admitted. I was able to see my family devastated for the first time: my mom, even though it seemed impossible for me, she was crying in my brother's arms, meanwhile my father was anxious walking from side to side.

I could see how worried he was, and for the first time I felt empathy, I saw how they actually cared about me, even if they didn't know how to show it. The truth is, we are all caught up in our own universe, myself included, lost and drowned in a selfish and inconsiderate world. I for example feel that nobody cares about me; I convinced myself I was not worthy, and little by little I realized I was wrong all along.

I closed my eyes to cry, and once I opened them again, I woke up in my hospital bed. It was night time. I would wake up over and over again, I couldn't differentiate between what was a dream and what wasn't... everything felt so real and lucid. I stood up from my bed and walked close to the boy laying one bed away from me; he looked so familiar, his face, just as the lady sleeping next to him. I took his hand and I felt a spark, like an electric reaction through the touch of our hands.

— That was... weird. Who are you? — I asked, I tried taking his hand again, this time there was no spark, and even though I can't explain it, I promise I felt something that I can't put into words.
— Was it you... in my dreams? — I sighted
— Are you okay, Amy? — The young lady asked. Immediately I dropped his hand and took a step back.
— How do you know my name? — I asked, confused.
— My name is Orly. I have been spending some time with

your parents these past couple of days. You want me to call them? — She asked.
— No — I said, very unfriendly and went back to my bed.

A FEW DAYS LATER...

I was ready to be discharged. I started packing my stuff to go back to the life I hated so much; these past few days in the hospital and the lucid dreams I had were just a little fleeting escape from my own reality, a consequence of a moment I can't remember at all. I tried to look at the positive side of it, but the idea of going back home and catching up with my daily routine didn't make me happy at all. I took my bags and as I was walking out of the ICU, a familiar voice interrupted me.

ORLY
You forgot something.

I looked at her, bitter and confused.

ORLY
(kindly)

Check underneath your pillow.

So I did, and there was a little blue book that had a picture of her son inside. of it.

I looked her straight in the eyes, speechless.

ANGELA
(loud)

Amy, hurry up. The car is ready.

I sighed and looked at the baby. Orly looked at me; she seemed to understand what I tried to say through my silence, I could see her eyes filled with nostalgia.

ORLY
It's okay. Go, keep it with you.
It will always take care of you.

I left and I didn't even care to ask for their names, or his name actually, but I think it didn’t matter, I was never going to see either of them again.

“We don’t need a name and a last name
to deeply know someone.
It’s enough with an interaction,
even if it is surreal.

I met him in my dreams
and that’s what truly matters.”`

CHAPTER 2.

SOMETIMES

"Dreams are part of an alternate reality surreal but for some ironic reason that word ends with the word 'real'."

NEW DAY, SAME LIFE.

The difference between yesterday and today is the way I play with time; for some reason I woke up making my past my present, lost in the memories of the dreams I had. I can't stop thinking about my parents and my brother crying for me at the hospital, I can't take that baby boy out of my head. What happened to him? Is he doing better?

All of a sudden my thoughts were interrupted: my mom entered my room, and for the first time we began to talk about what happened. My brother, Derek, entered right after her.

ANGELA

(serious)

Amy, we need to talk.

AMY

(avoiding Angela)

I was thinking we should all
go eat lunch, as a family.

Derek looked at me and sighed.

DEREK

(convinced)

I think it's a great idea, Ma.

ANGELA

Sounds good kids, but there is something we need to talk about first: your father and I. we were thinking that it would be best for you to study elsewhere.

AMY

What? But, why? Where? When? What for? Derek, do you agree on this?

My mother held me by the arm, trying to make a point.

ANGELA

So you can start over and set yourself free from this crazy stage we are going through. What happened is really serious, and your father and I fear that you might try it again if you stay.

AMY

(frustrated and desperate)

Try what, mom?

DEREK

(worried)

Hmmm, Sis, mom is right. What happened was really serious, and you need to have willpower. Although I don't think it's necessary to send her away.

AMY

Of course, because now I am a drug addict. I don't know how many times I have to tell you guys, I didn't take any drugs.

ANGELA

Amy, you don't have to lie anymore. We are trying to be understanding, you are a teenager and you have your own problems. We found a boarding school that has therapists on campus. It's one of the best schools in México. And you will be able to practice your Spanish. It would be like a summer camp, but… longer.

AMY

First of all: Mi español es perfecto. Second of all: Summer camp? Really?

Derek nodded, I could see he was convinced that I should go.

AMY

(hysterical)

This has to be a joke. I don't need a psychologist, much less Spanish classes.

DEREK

Deep down, I think it might work, sis.

(regretful)

No no, you know what mom? No, I don't think she should leave. I understand that what she did was wrong, but it's not her fault and I don't think the solution is to send her away instead of facing what's really going on between us as a family.

AMY

(relieved, and also ironic)

Finally…

ANGELA

(determined)

It's been decided, period.

AMY

(challenging)

Says who?

ANGELA

Your father and I spoke to a professional, and it's for the best.

AMY

(sarcastic)

Now you guys get along and make decisions together, nice.

ANGELA

(sighs)

Amy, this is not about us as a couple. It's about you and it's not something that is open for discussion. The decision has been made. You are leaving next week so you can start the semester with all the students.

DEREK

But, mom! This year isn't even over. She's gonna have to repeat the school year.

AMY

(shocked, ironic)

Of course, it's easier for you guys to send me away and continue with your lives. How would you feel if we sent you to rehab, mom?

ANGELA

This isn't about me, and I am a grown up woman and your mother so, show some respect.

AMY

Start respecting yourself and then you can ask others to respect you.

ANGELA
(furious)

Pack your stuff.

AMY
(sarcastic)

You can't force me.

ANGELA
Maybe if you were 18, but you're not. You are leaving and that is final.

AMY
(disappointed)

You want to know something funny? When I was at the hospital, I had a dream in which I saw you worried about me. From afar, you were actually sad and you looked like an actual family... United, I thought that was going to happen but all I see is the opposite.

Angela left the room, Derek sat next to me and hugged me.

DEREK
(sad)

I'm so sorry sis, I tried to convince them, but… they won't listen.

AMY
(sighs)

But, you do believe me, right?

DEREK
(sad)

It's not about what I believe or not, the test results were clear, you overdosed.

AMY

(frustrated)

It's all bullshit, I don't even know where to find drugs.

DEREK

(sad)

Don't tell me how, nor where, much less with who, because I'll kill them. Ok?

AMY

(hysterical)

Did you listen to what I said? I am telling you. I didn't do any drugs

DEREK

(sad)

You were about to die. How do you expect me to believe you?

AMY

I will show you they're wrong. I didn't do drugs, Derek.

DEREK

Good luck with that.

Derek left and my day was already ruined. I decided not to go to school, what for? I was leaving the country. What was the point of going to a school I wasn't going back to either way.

So I decided it was better to visit the baby at the hospital, I wanted to check up on him. I got there as fast as I could, but the nurses couldn't say much. Apparently the baby boy was sent home, but something tells me that was not good news.

I came back home to find my mom drowning herself in alcohol with depressive music at it's max volume, my brother didn't speak to me and, as usual, he was on his way out. My dad, of course… working. As far as myself, to not lose the habit, I walked straight to my room.

JUNE 20TH, 2008

I found myself dreaming with the baby again. This time, we were at a park full of balloons, pastel blue and he had a hat that said CONGRATULATIONS. I don't know if it was his birthday or what exactly, but what I do know is that lately, I am happier in my dreams that I am when I am awake. I know I said it's not relevant to know a person's life to get to know them deeply, but… at this point, I would like to know their names, or at least know if they're okay.

"Living a wonderful life in my dreams while sleeping in a world I don't belong to".

LATER THAT DAY

Meanwhile my life is all packed in one suitcase and I'm on my way to the airport: the day to "start over" is here, with a playlist full of sad songs to add a little nostalgia to my departure, and a backpack full of diverse emotions, and knots that accompany my solitude.

I was ready to leave. My flight was being announced and just as I was walking towards the gate I stumbled upon a guy about my age (and very handsome, just saying); it was really weird… I wasn't in the mood to socialize, but just like in the movies, when we stumbled, my documents and purse fell down, and this gave him time to introduce himself.

— Shit, I'm sorry. I didn't see you — he said.
— Don't worry, just try to not walk and text at the same time — I said, very rude.
— Well, well, well, are you this charming all the time? — he told me, as if he knew me from before.
— I'm sorry, I'm in a hurry — avoiding looking him in the eyes. As soon as we finished picking them up, we accidentally

touched each other and I felt a spark between us. Like an actual spark.
— Electricity... Sparks inside of me....— singing a song.
— Very funny — I said, staring at him.
— It's a song… — silent for a minute. — My name is Alberto, and you are?— he added, to break the silence.
— What? — I asked, out of content.

ALBERTO
Yea, it's Elton John's song…
(singing)
"Flying like a bird like electricity... electricity...and I'm free I'm free.."

He started singing the song in the middle of the airport. The truth is that his spontaneous personality impressed me; although he got a little shy when he saw I was staring at him.

ALBERTO
(breaking the ice)
I like your shoes!

AMY
Really? Weird, most people hate converse.

ALBERTO
Yeaaah, I'm not known for being part of the masses.

AMY
(sarcastic)
Ha ha, very funny… anyway. I have to go, they're calling in my flight.

ALBERTO
Mine too, but my gate has been changed. Where are you going?

AMY

Mexico.

ALBERTO

Seriously? Me too. Let's go, they changed it to gate 20.

I continued walking with a stranger that coincidentally had the same final destination as me. My trip started to make a little more sense, I don't know why but it felt like we had met before.

ALBERTO

What did you say your name was?

AMY

(half smiling)

Mmm.. Amy.

ALBERTO

Next time you smile, please let it be a full smile.

We were already lining up to get into the plane, I forgot to ask him about his seat. I walked to my seat in the 20th row and I didn't see him. I suppose he was seated in the back of the plane, but I didn't want to go after him. As we were about to depart, I didn't notice the seat next to mine was empty; and suddenly Alberto showed up from behind.

ALBERTO

(joking)

Uhg, Lacky is so annoying. He had to sit right next to you.

He moved his head doing a gesture for me to stand up and walked through, as if the seat was his.

AMY

Who's Lacky?

ALBERTO

Amy, Amy, Amy… you still need to spend more time with me.

(serious)

You need to learn how to speak sarcasm… no worries, no worries, I am the master of sarcasm, and you can teach me some Spanish, deal?

AMY

Is this your seat?

ALBERTO

I did a little arrangement with Lacky, told him you talked a little bit too much, and he's the type of guy that likes to be silent. You know.

AMY

You're crazy.

ALBERTO

That's the least of your worries, I've been told that before.

The truth is, Alberto was making my trip comfortable and unexpected; I even forgot I was going to Mexico to "start over". As soon as we landed I got a little panic attack filled with anxiety. Alberto had this peculiar way of looking at me in the eyes and make me feel at peace, I can't explain it, but there was something about his eyes that didn't allow me to see through them… but that wasn't necessarily a bad thing.

ALBERTO

What are you going to do in Mexico?

AMY

Well, since I'm not going to be seeing you again…

ALBERTO

Why not? Are you going to vanish or what?

AMY

Well, I'm going to a boarding school, in which I won't be able to come and go as I please… it's more or less the same.

ALBERTO

What if I kidnap you? I mean… who knows, maybe we'll run into each other again.

I remained silent.

ALBERTO

Soo.. you were saying?

AMY

I'm just going to that boarding school to learn Spanish.

He stared at me strangely, as if he already knew I was lying.

ALBERTO

(sarcastic)

Whatever lady, you'll come around with the whole story at some point. Let's go, vanishing girl.

AMY

Is this another one of your sarcastic jokes I'm supposed to understand?

ALBERTO

Damn, you're feisty , but yeah… You are a fast learner.

We walked out of the plane and got separated; a chauffeur from school was waiting for me, and as far as Alberto, well, I lost track of him inside the airport. I guess that the inefable and ephemeral moment of happiness in my new reality called "starting over" was over before it even started.

I got to what would be my home for the next year or so. Lucky me, my parents paid so I would have a room of my own; a lot of people would rather have roommates, but in my case I rather just live by myself, enjoying my solitude, something I am already used to

JUNE 21st, 2008.

My normal class schedule wouldn't start until August, so the deal my parents made was for me to go to therapy and summer activities and meet other students before the beginning of the year, including Spanish classes, which wasn't really necessary because my Spanish was on point. I learned by watching "La Familia Peluche" when I was little. I signed up for the Volleyball team, it's the only activity I actually like and my psychologist suggested that I join group activities to get involved in school. The training was good, I didn't become friends with anyone, neither did I make an effort to do so, but like in any high school… the three musketeers can't be missing, and can't take their eyes off of the new girl. I get it, I'm a stranger, foreign girl, and clearly I am not the hottest chick in school.

— ¿Cuál dijiste que era tu nombre? — one of them said, very arrogant.
— Sorry, what? — I couldn't hear what he said.
— Vaya, ¿no hablas Español entonces? — he continued speaking in Spanish, making fun of me along with two other jerks, throwing my bag to the floor in an attempt to scare me.
— Si lo hablo, así que… cualquier cosa que tengan que decir, lo voy a entender a la perfección — They were shocked when they realized that I actually spoke Spanish, but that didn't stop them from being bullies; finally a girl called them.
— Chicos, ¿vienen o qué? — Clearly the popular girl in school, and they walked straight towards her like the puppets they were; not without one last joke against me.
— Aguas, no somos muy receptivos con freaks como tú — he said, with a very offensive warning tone, and I just nodded.

They walked away and left me behind with all my stuff on the floor, as I started picking them up, a little nervous I must confess… I couldn't avoid thinking of the many times I was bullied at my old school, seems like my "starting over" mission was just a continuation translated into Spanish. I turned to a familiar voice:

AMY
What are you doing here?

ALBERTO
You can't hide how happy you are to see me. Look at you.

AMY
Shut up, but yes… can't deny it. What are you doing here?

ALBERTO
(enthusiastic)

I told you we would be seeing each other again; I saw your school card and I knew I would see you here. I came just for the summer to actually learn some Spanish, I can barely say 'Hola'. I just failed my first class, by the way.

AMY
Don't worry: I will help you with your Spanish, and you will help me have a bearable summer.

ALBERTO
We have to do something regarding that self esteem, I can't deal with that much negativity in my life.

AMY

Im sorry.

ALBERTO
(enthusiastic)

I'm just kidding, don't feel bad... although we do have to do something thing regarding your attitude towards life. Life is nothing but a beautiful thing called JOY.

He walked me to my room and left.

10:00 PM

My first day in that foreign hell was over, and I was actually happy to know that someone would keep me company, giving my life some color. I told my mom I would call her and tell her about my day, but I completely forgot, I spent the afternoon with Alberto and once I got to my room all I wanted to do was sleep. Tomorrow is a new day and also my first session with the therapist

"I am so excited, a space to remember how miserable I feel about my existence".

Yeah, that was all sarcasm.

CHAPTER 3

HOW DID I GET HERE?

JUNE 23RD.

I walked into the office and I was told to sit and wait until the Dr. arrived; I spent a few minutes alone and later on she walked in with a very imposing attitude which made me not like her at first sight.

— Tell me a little bit about you, Amy — she said, while sitting in her chair.
— Do I have to?— I asked.
— Whenever you're ready, no pressure — She said, haughty and challenging behind her Doctors coat.
I remained silent during the session until I saw her taking some notes in her notebook.

AMY
What are you writing? I haven't said a word.

PSYCHOLOGIST
Silence is also a form of expression.

AMY
I guess.

PSYCHOLOGIST
Would you like to play a game?

AMY
Seems like I have no other choice, do I?

PSYCHOLOGIST
I will ask you a few questions, and you will answer with the first thought that comes to mind. One word.

AMY

Mhm...

PSYCHOLOGIST

How do you feel about being in a new country?

AMY

Bored.

PSYCHOLOGIST

How do you feel most of the time?

AMY

Angry.

PSYCHOLOGIST

How would you describe your family?

AMY

Liars.

PSYCHOLOGIST

What do you think about life?

AMY

Breathing.

PSYCHOLOGIST

What's your passion?

AMY

Nonexistent.

PSYCHOLOGIST

Okay, good. How do you feel now?

AMY

Should I feel any different?

PSYCHOLOGIST

I understand, you have the right to feel the way you do, but you are here to get to know yourself. Don't waste that opportunity.

AMY

Okay, can I leave now?

PSYCHOLOGIST

We are done for the day. I will be seeing you tomorrow at the same time.

I walked out as fast as I could and once again, I ran over to Alberto, my things fell off my bag and coincidentally today I had both my diary and the blue little book the baby's mom gave me with his picture inside. Alberto, being a gentleman as always, picked up all my things, but not without feeling curious about the little blue book, he opened it right away. I was nervous about my diary, I didn't want him to read anything.

AMY

What are you doing here? Are you going to the same psychologist too? I am going to start thinking that you are stalking me.

He was skeptical reading the blue book that Orly gave me, and after a few seconds he spoke.

ALBERTO

Actually, I came to make sure that your psychologist didn't convince you to not hang out with me tonight for your first Shabbat ritual.

AMY

What?

ALBERTO

You are Jewish, right? I mean, you have a Zohar.

AMY

No, I'm not.

I took the book away from him and the baby's picture fell into his hands; he stared at it for a while.

ALBERTO

Mm, I see.. well let's say that I really like Jewish traditions. Who is Tito?

AMY

What? How do you know... wait.

ALBERTO

(showing the back of the picture)

It says it here.

AMY

Damn, it didn't cross my mind to look there.

ALBERTO

Why do you have a Zohar if you're not Jewish. Wierdo...

AMY

It's a long story.

ALBERTO

Good, we have all night to talk about it, over Shabbat dinner.

AMY

It's not even friday.

ALBERTO

Things are meant to be done in the present. I am a dreamer and I like to share the things I feel passionate about, and according to my beliefs, all we have is now. I don't want to wait for a Friday that may or may not come for you to have your first Shabbat experience with me. Let's see it as a rehearsal dinner, ok?

Alberto raised his arms victoriously happy and left.

ALBERTO

Don't bail on me.

I got really excited and ran into my room to get ready, but not before receiving a call from my mom after a few days of not talking.

ANGELA

(on the phone)

Hi sweetie, how have you been? How are you feeling?

AMY

I'm good, you know… getting used to this whole Spanish setting. And you?

ANGELA

I miss you a lot.

AMY

(sarcastic)

Sure.

ANGELA

I mean it, we miss you. But, tell me all

about it. How do you feel in your new school.

AMY

Same thing, different language.

ANGELA

Don't be like that, try opening up to your classmates.

AMY

Nothing to open up about mom, they're all jerks.

ANGELA

How was your new psychologist?

AMY

Also a jerk.

We shared an awkward silence for a few minutes, I felt bad, I could see she was worried.

AMY

I met a guy at the airport who happened to be coming to this school, but he is just here for summer school.

ANGELA

Awe, is he nice?

AMY

He's very nice, seems like a good friend. He invited to a Shabbat dinner tonight.

ANGELA

Shabbat?

AMY

Yes. He is a little crazy, but he's sweet and very funny.

ANGELA

I'm glad to know there is someone there for you.

AMY

Yes. Well, I have to go mom, I want to clean my room a bit and then get ready.

I hung up with my mom and layed down holding the Zohar and Tito's picture; I was emotionally tired, but I couldn't stop wondering how he was doing. I wanted to know what happened to him, why was he at the hospital. I told Alberto I would be at his place at 5 p.m, but I fell asleep.

I suddenly woke up in a garden, nobody around. I started hearing someone laughing, and all of a sudden I saw him, it was him running around a foggy pool, playing with a soccer ball. I saw him from afar.

— Tito? — I asked. And I felt someone grabbing my hand, it was him next to me. We were both looking at his other self from afar, playing around the pool.
— Your name is Tito, right? — I asked. He agreed moving his head and smiled.

Out of nowhere, everything turned grey and I saw him drowned in the pool. A man, whom I supposed was his father, jumped into the pool to save him; I saw everything happening at the same time, everyone around him was crying and running asking for help. His father would do CPR on him, but he was unresponsive. The maid got him a towel and I could see all of them crying out of desperation. Orly entered, I remembered her face, it was her. She grabbed him rapidly and ran towards the car.

Tito grabbed me by the hand and it was like traveling through time and space: we went from being in a garden and a pool in the middle of all the chaos, to a hospital emergency room. I could see with my own eyes how they were trying to resuscitate him, and I was next to him. I understood it all, we both died and all of a sudden both our hearts began to beat again, at the same time; I could see the pain in his mom's eyes… she wasn't crying, but I could see how her world was falling apart just by looking at her eyes. Behind her… at the end of a hospital's hallway I saw my mom and my brother standing there.

I could see everything that happened while I was unconscious, from another perspective. I know it sounds crazy, because this is just a dream, but… I think there is something more to them, because I keep having them over and over again, from a different point of view, from another perspective, but always the same message.

I woke up after one last electroshock and the backsound of two hearts beating strong, with my eyes full of tears. I wanted to call my mom, but my phone was full of messages from Alberto, it was past our dinner time. I dressed up as fast as I could and ran out the door. I got to Alberto's apartment, he also had one for himself.

AMY

I guess you don't like roommates?

ALBERTO

(sarcastic)

Hi Alberto, what a beautiful room you have.

AMY

Idiot, you got my point.

ALBERTO

Let's put it this way: I like my privacy.

AMY

I can tell, if we point out the fact that I am your only friend and the only person you talk to. I get it. I have a room of my own too.

ALBERTO

Thank you for the confirmation, I knew that already.

AMY

Ha ha! Very funny, thank you. Always so cute.

He took the orange juice bottle I bought, and I don't know why but a flashback from the dream I had with Tito crossed my mind and my eyes got watery.

ALBERTO

(worried)

Are you okay?

AMY

Yeah… no, uhm. I need to ask you something, and please don't tell me I'm crazy because that is public knowledge, I need you to take me seriously.

ALBERTO

(bluffing)

That is a challenge, but I'll try. What's up?

AMY

I've been having dreams, but they seem so real… like, if I was on a different dimension and my subconscious was trying to show me an alternate reality, something from my past.

ALBERTO

Why do you think that?

AMY

I don't know… this is the thing, the baby from the picture: I met him at the hospital. Well, First, I met him in my dreams and then when I woke up, he was in a bed next to mine.

ALBERTO

And you were in the hospital because?

AMY

I fell and hit my head, got a concussion.

ALBERTO

And the baby? Tito, right?

AMY

Well, I just had a dream about him. I was walking with him next to me holding my hand and he showed me what happened, but I don't know if it's real or if it's just a dream. I've been asking myself the same thing for a few days now and… I don't know, these dreams seem like the answer.

ALBERTO

I see…

(thoughtful)

I believe in the power of dreams. They are complex, sometimes… but they usually have a message that we might

or might not understand the morning after, but through life we find ourselves understanding them, step by step, in different circumstances. I think before understanding what happened to him, you must accept what happened to you.

AMY

What do you mean?

(nervous)

I told you, I fell.

ALBERTO

Amy, I'm not talking about you having an accident, or falling, or whatever… I'm talking about what happened inside of you and how it changed you.

AMY

Please explain.

ALBERTO

What do you think about life?

AMY

My psychologist asked the same thing.

ALBERTO

What did you say?

AMY

Overrated, meaningless, we are just breathing.

ALBERTO

(bluffing)

401 unauthorized ERROR, dear Amy.

AMY

What? Why?

ALBERTO

Because many of us can't breathe and yet we are alive, while others breathe and walk free, but are dead inside.

AMY

I don't understand.

ALBERTO

It's a metaphor, Amy. Find the life you lost within your soul, in your dreams… you have a mission to fulfill.

AMY

Wow… You took the role seriously.

ALBERTO

And… you killed the moment, dumbass. And by the way, its WAO, not 'wow'.

AMY

I'm sorry, I'm not used to having these types of conversations.

ALBERTO

What about your therapist?

AMY

I don't like her.

ALBERTO

Do you like someone? Other than me.

AMY

Not that I know of.

He cracked laughing, and started eating. We had a good time. He told me everything about Jewish traditions that I had no clue about; he read a paragraph of the Zohar Tito's mom gave me, and explained what it was.

ALBERTO
You are very lucky: a gift like this is not given often, much less to a stranger.

AMY
I know, I mean… I don't speak Hebrew, but that book gives me peace, somehow… I don't know why, but it feels good.

ALBERTO
Some connections transcend life, Amy.

I half smiled at him and remained silent. I took my phone out and snapped a picture of us, sent it to my mom.

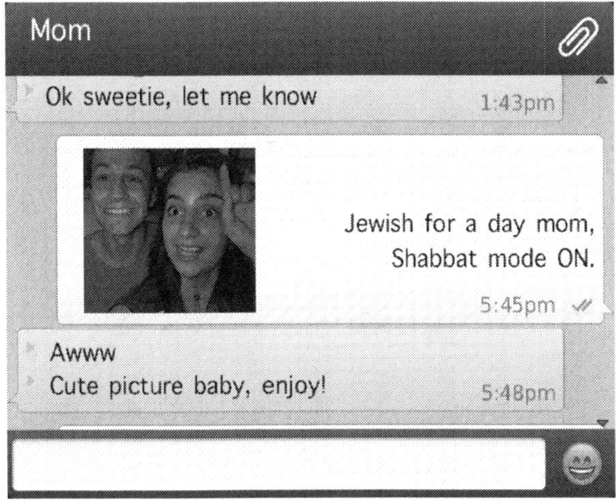

CHAPTER 4

MY TRUTH

JULY 1ST, 2008

Tito and I were walking holding hands once again in a park full of blue balloons; as always, he was smiling and I was just standing there, trying to understand the setting. I was still confused and couldn't figure out the meaning of these dreams… the only thing I knew for sure was that there was something he was trying to show me. We walked together and entered my house in San Francisco; my parents were in the kitchen, and I could hear them talking about splitting up.

ANGELA

I want you to leave, Jaime.

JAIME

Let's try to fix this, I don't want us to break up.

ANGELA

Break up? Jaime, this is not a boyfriend/girlfriend converstion. You decided to disrespect me when you left with that whore.

JAIME

It's not like that, there is no one else.

ANGELA

You sure?

JAIME

Of course I am.

ANGELA

(hysterical)

If you really want to stay, and fix this… for me and the kids, fire her.

My dad looked at her doubtful.

JAIME
Don't make this about the kids.

ANGELA
Don't change the subject.

JAIME
Why don't you take a deep breathe, calm down and we'll continue this later?

ANGELA
Either you fire her, or you start packing up your things.

JAIME
Fine Angela, fine. I'll sign her resignation first thing tomorrow morning.

My mom sat quietly, victorious and my dad left the scene, angry.

JAIME
I hope this makes you happy.

We transitioned from my kitchen to Tito's house, in which he showed me his family; they were all having breakfast together, Tito included. I could see how happy they were, how much they enjoyed each other's company, but from one second to the next everything changed: Orly, was standing in the kitchen, Tito wasn't in his high chair anymore and his siblings seemed sad, as of his dad, I could see the frustration in his eyes. I felt bad… I realized Tito was holding my hand, and he pulled me to keep walking.

We started walking and ended up in a hospital, I saw him lying on a bed attached to tubes and machines that kept him "alive", if "breathing through a machine" can be called life. In that room, Orly was standing next to a doctor.

DOCTOR

Orly, the kid is in a deep coma, in a very delicate state. After the accident his brain spent too much time without oxygen due to lack of heartbeats when you were driving him to the hospital.

ORLY

I understand that, Dr. but I did some research. The Stem cell treatment, I couldn't find anyone who can do it where I live, you are the best neurologist in the country.

DOCTOR

I know, but as I told you over the phone: it is an extremely expensive treatment and statistically speaking it only works in 1 out of 50 patients. You son is in no condition to receive the treatment.

ORLY

Please, Doctor, at least try it. He revived, he was dead when we found him and his heart started beating again after 12 minutes without breathing. Please.

DOCTOR

I'm sorry.

I was so frustrated listening to the doctor refusing to give Tito a chance to live, and there was nothing I could do. Why was it so hard for that doctor to at least run some tests and see if he qualified. He was only talking based on the file case, he wasn't really trying and I could see Orly's eyes lost with devastation, it broke my heart. I couldn't understand how the life of a three year old baby was being taken, without him wanting to.

I woke up agitated, sweaty and angry. Ran straight to the bathroom and couldn't stop looking at my reflection.

"All I could feel was hate, because I was the one that got a second chance; he didn't, he didn't even get the chance to understand the true meaning of life".

JULY 4tH, 2008.

Another day, another appointment, another day to breathe in questions and exhale empty answers… at the psychologist.

PSYCHOLOGIST
How are you feeling?

AMY
Whatever, as usual.

PSYCHOLOGIST
Have you made any new friends?

AMY
(smily)

Yes, Alberto.

PSYCHOLOGIST
You like him?

AMY
(shy)

Ew, no. We're just friends.

PSYCHOLOGIST
Okay, that's fine. Tell me more about him.

AMY
He's very kind, and fun. Not like other guys; with him I can feel he wants a true friendship without an agenda or sexual intentions. He listens.

PSYCHOLOGYST
Good, I'm glad to hear that, Amy. How do you feel about playing the same

game we played last time?

AMY

I don’t understand the purpose of it, but okay.

PSYCHOLOGIST

You already know, the first word that comes to mind.

AMY

Yup.

PSYCHOLOGYST

How are you feeling?

AMY

Accompanied.

PSYCHOLOGIST

How is your family?

AMY

Borken.

PSYCHOLOGIST

What can you do to fix that?

AMY

Nothing.

PSYCHOLOGIST

Why?

AMY

It’s not my responsibility.

PSYCHOLOGIST

Those were four words, but good. You

see?

AMY

What?

PSYCHOLOGIST

You let yourself get affected by problems that are not yours, much less your fault. And you end up loaded with emotional crap that doesn't belong to you. Without deeply thinking about it, you know deep down those are not your problems to fix and that there is nothing you can do to fix them, it's on them and their desire to keep breaking their relationship or fixing it.

AMY

What am I supposed to do then? Act like I know nothing and ignore it?

PSYCHOLOGIST

No, Amy. But don't blame yourself, because it's not your fault.

AMY

What do I do then?

I stood silent, thoughtful and for the first time I could see things as how they really were. I felt relieved, I sighed and it felt like I was letting go of a huge load in my back.

I told Alberto we would meet up at fivr. I had a few hours of free time before meeting with him, but I decided to go to the coffee shop where we said we would meet, I wanted to write a little bit; I spent several days trying to write something in my journal, things I have in my mind, my emotions have intensified lately and I wanted to leave that in writing in case rebellious Amy decides to act on again in the future. I was reading my diary, drawing and trying to connect some things that made my mind feel overwhelmed and that I hadn't been able to talk to anyone about, suddenly Alberto scared me from behind.

AMY

(agitated)

You effing idiot. How dare you? You almost killed me.

ALBERTO

You have to be aware of your surroundings, Amy. I could have been a thief.

AMY

Shut up, we are in a school with a lot of security, as you can see.

ALBERTO

What is that? Poetry?

Alberto took the diary.

ALBERTO

(reading out loud)

It seems incredible to me how dreams can introduce us to people we have never met; sometimes they don't even have a face, but I have entered into an alternate reality that is completely lucid, or so it seems. I walk lost in my reality and I find myself in my dreams, looking for clues that I do not know if they are there; I don't know if one day I will get the answers I'm looking for but, what is the purpose of a dream? Is it a state of your subconscious showing you things that you want to happen? That can happen, that will happen, or that are happening at that precise moment? Or perhaps they have already passed: thoughts, desires, or your own imagination wanting to answer questions that you don't dare to ask out loud. But how is all this connected to reality? Or do we dream because we want to live in an alternate one? If so, then what is the purpose of a nightmare? I don't know, but what I do know is that I am a teenager trying to understand the images of my dreams in which the protagonist is a three year old boy.

ALBERTO
(shocked)
Did you write this?

AMY
Yes.

ALBERTO
Damn young lady, have you shared this with anyone else?

AMY
No, are you crazy?

ALBERTO
It's really good, like... reaaaally.

AMY
No, it's only for me, give it back.

ALBERTO
You selfish little… Amy. You should

share your AHA moment with the world, not everybody reaches that point and sometimes it's necessary to have a little boost from someone else.

AMY

Huh? What are you talking about?

ALBERTO

Come on Amy, you would be a hit. A blog: *TheVanishedGirl.com* and upload your writings, you would be the next J.K Rowling.

AMY

You are hallucinating, give it back, Alberto, please.

ALBERTO

Fine. But it's a shame, you could help others by posting things like this, even yourself.

AMY

(sighs)

Remember what I told you the other day? About my dreams and the hospital?

ALBERTO

The one in which you were dying because a vampire was sucking your blood?

AMY

HA HA, very funny.

ALBERTO

What? They are real.

AMY

I'm serious.

ALBERTO

Yeah, me too. But okay. I do remember, what now?

AMY

I lied: it wasn't a dream, nor an accident.

ALBERTO

I know.

AMY

How? What do you mean? What do you know?

ALBERTO

I don't know anything, I just connected the dots: psychologist, moving to a foreign country "to start over", I figured something happened and you needed to run away from it, I just didn't want to ask.

AMY

Mmmm...

ALBERTO

Listen, you don't have to tell me everything. Whatever happened made you who you are, and you are the only one with the power to turn your negative experiences into positive outcomes. It's your decision.

AMY

But how? I haven't even been able to

understand it myself.

ALBERTO

The way I see it is that fear gives you the opportunity to face everything and rise, or forget everything and run… You are one decision away from what you want to be, but only if you believe in yourself.

AMY

But, I can't… not on my own.

ALBERTO

That's the problem, you think you can't. And the solution to that is to tell you that you're not alone, at all.

AMY

Nobody listens to me, I have never been able to talk about this with anyone.

ALBERTO

A-L-B-E-R-T-O, repeat after me: ALBERTO, I'm not "nobody".

I was breathless at that time after all the laughter.

AMY

I meant my family, fool. You don't even know what happened; maybe when you find out you'll believe I'm crazy and run away.

ALBERTO

Try to see beyond what meets the eye, Amy. Life is so much more than breathing.

AMY
I know, and it makes sense... I guess.

ALBERTO
You don't have to tell me anything, as I said. Just accept it, and the day you feel completely secure to share it, whether it's with me or a rock, I'll be here. Never forget that, life is in constant evolution and we always live experiences that will change our lives forever.

Alberto stood up from the table and looking at me straight in the eyes, he slowly put the notebook in front of me.

ALBERTO
If I were you, I would pick up my broken pieces and turn them into art, instead of beating myself up with the fact that I let others get to me. You already started, don't underestimate yourself.

Alberto hugged me and I lost myself in my own thoughts.

AMY
Where are you going?

ALBERTO
Tengo clases de español.

AMY
Vayaaaa vaya, pero escúchate.

ALBERTO
Yeah, yeah, whatever...

AMY

Eres un gran amigo, Alberto.

ALBERTO

I have no idea what you just said, but I will ask my teacher. In case it was something nice, then: Gracias; if not. We have a meeting under the pool after my class.

He left to class and I stayed there a little longer, I was inspired to write and then I left to my room. I had to wake up early in the morning.

JULY 7TH, 2008.

I woke up in a boys room in which Tito was laying down. I concluded it was his bedroom. I saw him attached to machines all over his body, a nurse would walk in and out. The Tito of my dreams wasn't walking with me this time: I was on my own walking around his house. His seven year old brother walked in and Orly was right behind him, but she stood by the door.

ORLY

Be careful, Sam. Don't disconnect anything.

SAM

I'm going to show him a game.

Sam started playing with threads, making figures with them; he showed them to Tito as if he was awake playing with him. He made the figure of the Eiffel Tower, then of a bridge, while talking to him and explaining how each figure was made. Orly left the room, and I stood at the door watching Sam play with Tito.

SAM

(whispering to Tito)

I don't know if you can hear me but... you know little bro? We miss you running around the house. You should wake up soon, mommy cries a lot at night. We love you. We need you.

Sam kissed Tito in the forehead and left the room; I followed him and I transitioned to the park where I always meet with Tito. As always, there he was, playing around, running and jumping, and having fun, smiling: as if he knew that he had the power to make me feel at peace just by watching him how much he enjoys being alive after the pain I felt after seeing him lying in his bed, almost dead. Tito sat in the grass surrounded with a lot of crayons and blank paper.

He started drawing, and just a few seconds later he surprised me with a gift, it was a childish style drawing of his family; a tear fell down my face and suddenly I woke up, but not in my reality, I woke up in an empty white space, alone… Tito wasn't there anymore, but I still had the drawing he gave me in the park.

Everything was spinning around me and the sound of a heartbeat machine started beating in my head, it was a loud flat line, the deadly line.I couldn't stand it; I could also listen to desperate voices screaming in the back.

SAM

Mom, why is he shaking like that?

(desperate)

Help him, please.

I faded back to Tito's bedroom and I saw him having a seizure; the nurses were working on him, doing their best… and there he was, Tito holding my hand as a hologram, as if his presence in my dreams depended on the flat line of the heartbeat machine.

I was crying desperately, I was afraid that he was going to die; I couldn't understand what was actually happening and it killed me listening to the pain and suffering in his brother's voice. A white ray of light blinded my eyes and I woke up agitated. I went straight to the bathroom with nausea but I didn't vomit, I just washed my face and looked at myself in the mirror, lost myself for a few seconds… and then I sat in my desk thinking about the dream, took my diary and began to write.

"It's been two weeks since I got here and I haven't been able to f it in. I still cry at night, I'm still the same unhappy girl who left home. Alberto became my guardian angel, and the idea of him leaving at the end of the summer kills me. I don't feel ready to be on my own, however I have Tito in my dreams, telling me a story that I still can't put together, but he has this unique way of making me smile, even if it comes with nostalgia, he shares his happiness with everyone nostalgia, he shares his happiness with everyone regardless of what his family is going through.

I lost track of time writing on my diary, and my phone rang. I picked up.

AMY

Hi mom! How are you?

ANGELA

I'm good sweetie, and you? How is everything there?

AMY

All good. Just woke up. I have to go to therapy in a few minutes, then I have to go to Volleyball practice. How are things at home?

ANGELA

(sad)

Actually, I was calling to talk to you about that.

AMY

(sighs)

What's new?

ANGELA

You dad and I are getting a divorce.

AMY

It's okay.

ANGELA

(impressed)

Oh… wow… are you okay? I mean, we are going to be okay, it's for the best baby.

AMY

(nostalgic)

I understand, whatever decision you guys make, I'll get it. As long as you are both happy. I will be too.

ANGELA

Really?

AMY

Yeah, I mean… it's not like there is something I can do about it, it's your relationship.

"It hit me, I understood sometimes I won't be able to fix a problem regardless of what I say or feel, in this case, I am a third party in my parent's relationship: whatever I say

or whatever I do, the final decision is up to them. Together or apart, they will continue to be my parents, and I will continue to be their daughter, and I know they will always be there for me… even if they don't know how to show their love sometimes, even if they make mistakes, we are all human and failing is part of life. I also understood that there are some things not even the psychologist nor Alberto could answer, but they can listen… and sometimes that's enough, especially now that I have learned to express myself, at least more than I used to. My therapy session was okay, nothing important honestly, but I left the Dr's office and went straight to Alberto's place to tell him everything, and for the first time I wasn't ashamed to say it out loud".

I knocked on Alberto's door desperately. I don't know why I was feeling so eager to talk about it. He opened the door, in his pajamas. He was surprised to see me, and I was surprised to seem him in pajamas with fish prints on it.

ALBERTO

(sarcastic)

Awe, I thought it was the pizza.

AMY

(confused and a bit lost)

What?

ALBERTO

It's too late for jokes, my bad.

AMY

Whatever… I'm ready.

ALBERTO

Ready for what? I am not, I just want to stay here and watch TV all day.

AMY

(takes a deep breath)

To tell you everything.

ALBERTO

(laughing)

Ohhhh… of course, I forgot we had a therapy session. My bad, my bad.

AMY

(nervous)

Don't judge okay? I have accepted who I am and what happened.

ALBERTO

Before you begin… I want you to know that I would never judge you. You became my best friend; we met not too long ago, I know, but you are special and I have noticed your change from who you were when I met you, to who you are today. You have evolved.

AMY

Ehh.. two months ago, nice.

ALBERTO

Time is an illusion, Amy, but whatever that's a different story. Focus. Tell me.

AMY

I'm epileptic.

ALBERTO

Right, that explains the mysterious pills in your purse.

AMY

Are you spying on me?

ALBERTO

I pay attention Darling, there is a difference. Plus I have to be prepared if something happens.

I was very confused as to why he would know so much about me

ALBERTO

Let's say I did some research on the pills.

AMY

Creep. Whatever, as I was saying… I had a seizure and my mom found me in the bathroom floor with a concussion and that led me to a respiratory attack and I woke up in the hospital two days later. That's when I started dreaming with the baby.

ALBERTO

Tito?

AMY

Damn, you do pay attention, f*ck.

ALBERTO

Told you.

(proud of himself)

Is that it?

AMY

Yes, I think, mm I don't know. I still

can't remember a lot of things.

ALBERTO

You're not ready, I get it.

AMY

I just don't remember a few things… it's like i have gaps I can't seem to remember.

ALBERTO

What do you remember?

I sighed hopeless and shameful.

ALBERTO

Maybe if you talk about it you'll remember.

AMY

(nervous and ashamed)

May 15th I lost my virginity to a boy who was supposed to be my boyfriend.

ALBERTO

"Supposed to be"... what does that mean?

AMY

It's complicated, everything was like... secretly. He didn't like to be seen with me so he convinced me to keep things between the two of us.

ALBERTO

And you agreed?

AMY

(ashamed)

Yes, I didn't think it was a big deal. We spent most of our time together, just not in school.

ALBERTO

You mean, not in front of his friends?

AMY

Aham...

ALBERTO

Okay, I get it. Sorry for what I am about to say but you are stupider than I thought, and him... well, he is a dick.

AMY

He's a dude.

ALBERTO

Hey!

AMY

You're different.

ALBERTO

(bragging)

I know, one of a kind. So, what else happened?

AMY

Well, that day Frank went to my place and... you know. We had... we did it. And it was okay, but he left right away. And the day after, I heard him talking to his friends at school.

ALBERTO

What were they talking about?

I broke into tears and remembered it as if it were yesterday.

AMY

He was friends with some dudes that would say I was a lesbian, and as much as I would try to not pay attention, it was hard. Especially because Frank would not step up for me, defend me... you know? On the contrary. But, I remember it all, they were talking about me as if I was a piece of garbage.

FRANK

(bragging)

I'm telling you bro, it wasn't that bad... I just told myself it wasn't her, plus... it was dark.

FRIEND

(laughing)

I can't believe you banged her.

FR ANK

(threatening him)

Shut up, this is between us. It was just a bet, you hear me?

FRIEND

(pushing frank backwards)

Take it easy, I'm not saying any- thing. You think I want anyone to know that my best friend had sex with a lesbo? Fuck no. How much did you bet?

FR ANK

Enough to be able to take Alison on a real date.

FRIEND

I hope so bro, foreal... just look at her, if it wasn't because you fucked her, I would keep on thinking she's gay.

AMY

(talking to Alberto)

I remember walking towards them, just so Frank could see me... and all they did was laugh. I ran away from them and went straight to the bathroom. I spent the whole day crying. When I got home I had no one to talk to; after that I can't re- member anything else honestly. I guess it's something I don't want to remember. It was always like that in school, everyone thought I was gay, and all I would hear would be rumors after rumors.

ALBERTO

I am sorry, so sorry.

AMY

It's not your fault. I would have liked to meet you before; I'm sure you would have stopped me from doing it.

ALBERTO

Honestly, yes. If I were you, I would have liked to meet me before too.

AMY

I guess.

ALBERTO

Amy, listen. Nothing is your fault. I mean, it is but just a little bit. You gave him the power to use you, but at the age of 15... what do we really know? And that's okay. Everything.

AMY

You are so mature sometimes it scares the crap out of me.

ALBERTO

HEY! I'm always mature, I just like to joke around... it gives me a sense of humor that makes me, me.

AMY

You are amazing, like some sort of... I don't know... an angel.

ALBERTO

Please don't fall in love with me, we are already way in to deep in the friendzone.

AMY

Ewww, shut up. I say that because you're different. I feel you are a real friend, unconditional... you know? With no intentions beyond that.

ALBERTO

What does "unconditional" mean to you?

AMY

Wow, that is a.... Deep meaningful question.

ALBERTO

You are not allowed to die, yet... faded girl. Well, I mean: you are not allowed to fade, yet.

AMY

We are all going to die at some point, right?

ALBERTO

Not before you find your WAO and your AHA.

AMY

What do you mean?

ALBERTO

Have you ever felt that sense of admiration when you learn something new? Like, when someone shares an experience or some- thing you have no idea about and it impacts you at a level that changes your whole perspective in life and you get the chills and your heart beats so fast that you can hear it? And suddenly you whisper “wao” to yourself, only you can hear it. And in that moment your eyes shine so bright that they reveal the moment of impact, it doesn’t matter the person, or the solitude. All that matters is that brief moment of impact that leads you to your first step of evolution.

AMY

Wao...

ALBERTO

Something like that, but deeper.

AMY

And the AHA moment?

ALBERTO

It's different for everyone. I haven't found mine, yet. But I know you will find yours and you will feel it so deep within you that you will yell at the world and everyone will stare at you as if you were some crazy person, but you will not be able to hide it, much less be afraid of it... so strong that you are going to feel the need to share it. Sometimes it's excitement, some- times it's nostalgia with a bit of happiness... it all depends, I haven't been able to find mine.

AMY

But, what is it?

ALBERTO

It's everything, Amy.

AMY

Please be more specific.

ALBERTO

Let yourself be surprised and stop asking so many questions. The point of what I just said is that you are not allowed to die before finding that moment, okay?

AMY

And you are not allowed to leave when the summer ends.

ALBERTO
Let's see how you behave these
next few weeks.

He drank what was left of the bottle of coke. We had a good time, as always when it comes to spending time with Alberto. But for the first time I questioned our friendship, I realized I don't know anything about him regarding his family, or his personal life... where is he from? What does his parents do for a living? What's his last name? I wanted to know more about him, but honestly I decided to go. I had a tough day, emotionally and even though I digested the news better than expected, I still had to process the whole idea of them getting a divorce, like: the moment I go back home they'll be living in different houses.

The following morning I woke up with a message from my brother, and one from Frank. Random as F*ck, I know. It's been a while since I spoke to either of them. I haven't really reached out to them, neither have them.

I smiled at both messages and I understood what Alberto meant by "unconditional love" and the difference between that and "just love".

Frank

Down for a second round?

Derek

Sup little sis, I know we haven't spoken much lately, but I wanted to tell you that I miss you, and I'm here for you whenever you need. You are my favorite person in the world and I will always love you; no matter what you do or what I do or say. Love you forever — Your big brother.

LOVE

Thank you for being the one who fills my heart with illusion every day.

Thank you for being the one who allows me to sleep at peace every night.

Thank you for being the one who keeps me moving forward. For being the definition of what it means to be alive.

Thank you for being the strength that leads my path. For letting me fall, so that I can rise once more.

That's you, dear love.

The thing you see at night, and what you feel within. The motive for the most beautiful songs, and even those not as beautiful.

You are the one who inspires the letters that become poetry.

And you are not always a synonym of sex.

But your meaning is always truth.

You always walk in front of us, and when you don't you hold us from behind.

You land in our lives to surprise us, when we least expect you, but one day, sooner or later you say hello.

I am your witness, love.

You are the most uncertain feeling there is, and certainly without measure at all.

However, sometimes you are just that: love.

Meaning brevity, and you stop by just to say hello.

And leave without saying goodbye.

And then I understand, there are other types of love.

UNCONDITIONAL LOVE

The one who sometimes hurts, but never leaves.

The one who challenges any circumstances and don't care about what people say.

The one who lives within very few of us and walks through life being taken for granted.

The one we appreciate the least, and yet never controls, usually misunderstood, and the one who gets the blame without understanding it doesn't matter how much wrong you do, it will always be love.

The company your demons get, who pushes you to love them, to stop blaming them and start to embrace them.

The one who teaches reality as positive and negative:
the one who makes you human, who gives you the essence that defines you.

The one who shows you the real path towards love, especially the one who teaches you that letting go is a proof of true love.

That's who you are, sometimes distant, sometimes absent, synonym of truth, the purest form of love, the forever type.

You are:

from the verb TO BE.

And from that time,
you are the correct grammar.

That's you, unconditional love.
Now I want to ask you, reader:

Are you love? Or unconditional love?

It's fine if you're not both, nor is good or bad, but it's always good to know.

That way you will know, where to stay and when to go.

"YOU ARE GOING TO FEEL THE NEED TO SHARE YOUR PURPOSE WITH THE UNIVERSE."

CHAPTER 5

WAO

ANOTHER DAY IN THERAPY

It was just another day, same routine, same feeling, but I must admit, something was different within me. I was talking a little bit more, at least for me it was a lot, but of course my therapist didn't think it was enough.

PSYCHOLOGIST
How are you feeling today, Amy?

AMY
Why do you always ask the same question?

PSYCHOLOGIST
Because it's a new day, and we always get to feel different every day. I want to know how are you feeling today.

AMY
I'm okay, better... I feel better.

PSYCHOLOGIST
Why do you think it's so hard for you to express yourself?

AMY
I'm not very expressive, I guess.

PSYCHOLOGIST
How is your friend?

AMY
Alberto?

PSYCHOLOGIST
Yes, can I see him? He seems to be the only person that makes you smile.

AMY

Not just him, Tito as well.

PSYCHOLOGIST

Who is Tito?

AMY

Uhm...the baby from the hospital.

PSYCHOLOGIST

We have not spoken about him, we can, if you want to.

I took out my phone and showed her a picture of Alberto, to avoid going deeper into the conversation about Tito, but she didn't say anything about the picture.

PSYCHOLOGIST

Would you like to recap your visit to the hospital?

AMY

(avoiding)

I had a seizure and a concussion.

PSYCHOLOGIST

You sound angry.

AMY

I am. I don't understand why I got better and Tito didn't. It's not fair.

PSYCHOLOGIST

What's unfair?

AMY

That I lived, and Tito didn't.

PSYCHOLOGIST
Why do you think it's unfair that you lived?

AMY
I don't know, it doesn't matter anymore.

PSYCHOLOGIST
You life matters. Amy, not all accidents have the same ending. Yours wasn't as bad as his, you have a condition that can be con- trolled with medicine.

AMY
It's not a condition, it's a consequence.

PSYCHOLOGIST
Tell more about Tito, so I can understand better.

AMY
There is not much I can say; I never met him. We shared ICU's. His mom gave me a gift when I was leaving the hospital and ever since then, I've been having dreams about him.

PSYCHOLOGIST
What type of dreams?

AMY
I don't know how to explain it... but I see him and his family, the accident.

PSYCHOLOGIST
Why do you think it's happening to you?

AMY

I don't know okay? I'm just pissed because I got better and he didn't. He was only 3 years old, he hasn't even been able to ask himself what life is.

PSYCHOLOGIST

Since when do you have seizures? Did you inherited it?

I started hyperventilating and crying; I told her what Tito showed me in my dreams and the session ended with me talking about it.

As an exercise she told me to close my eyes and take a deep breath... Suddenly I found myself next to Orly, she was talking to the Dr. It was like a follow up of the one time the Dr. was denying Tito the Stem cell treatment.

His heart stopped beating and all I could hear was the loud flat line, and there he was, Tito was now next to me and grabbed my hand. I finally understood why he showed up in my dreams: *everytime he was about to die he would guide me through to understand what was going on and give me an answer to my "why's"*, even though at that moment it didn't make sense to his family.

Tito was in cardiac arrest while he was repeatedly telling Orly he was not going to proceed with the Stem Cell Treatment. Everything was unclear, a few doctors and the nurses were doing everything to bring him back. I was feeling Orly's pain just by staring at her eyes. I laid on my knees:

AMY

Please go back.

He was crying and he would close his eyes so strong, he didn't want to see himself go through that. For the first time he hugged me... really really strong, as if he was afraid of me letting go. I saw Orly's face and everything was in slow motion, the doctor's face changed completely, Tito's heart beat again and he vanished from my arms.

DOCTOR
I'll give the order to run the right tests and see if he is a fit for the treatment. I'm not promising anything, ma'm. But I will try.

ORLY
Orly, please. Call me Orly.

DOCTOR
Okay, Orly. I also need your husband to sign the papers.

ORLY
Yes, of course. I will call him right away.

DOCTOR
Do it quick, before I change my mind.

ORLY
Thank you so much Dr, in the name of my family, thank you.

Orly cleaned her face, laid next to Tito and kissed him on the forehead over and over again.

ORLY
We need you, my baby. You will be back, I know that. You have to come back.

I woke up and it was 2 AM. I grabbed my phone to call Alberto. I didn't want to be alone. I needed his company to pro- cess everything I just saw, and the whole idea of letting go of the idea of Tito living in my dreams forever was spinning in my head, because even though he would show me things that made me cry, he would also teach me life lessons no other human being has been able to, but what I love the most, is the moment he smiles and laughs, running all over the park.

He gave me the opportunity to see life and death, but I knew deep down in my heart I had to let him go so he could go back to his family, I just wasn't sure if I was ready to let him go.

Alberto knocked on my door faster than I thought, and as soon as he walked in I hugged him and broke into tears.

ALBERTO

(walking into the apartment)

Hello hello... VIP delivery, personal therapyst please dial 1800 ALBERTO.

AMY

Please never change.

ALBERTO

(cheering me up)

It's because of those tears that I decided to bring sodas with the logo hidden, just so it would look like beer and pretend we are old enough to drink, even though we live in a country were you can go to war at 18 but can't drink until you are 21. Anyways, special beer delivery to my dear friend.

I couldn't avoid to smile. He hugged me and kissed me in the forehead.

ALBERTO

Spill the tea. Listen, this is the last free session, especially at this time of the night.

AMY

Mhum.

ALBERTO

I'm serious. What's up?

AMY

Please promise you will never leave me.

ALBERTO

(worried)

What happened? Why are you acting like this?

AMY

My dreams... Everytime Tito shows up I see him dying, sometimes he is alive with his family, happy, celebrating the gift of life but then he shows up next to me, and this one made me understand that he is only allowed to touch me when something is happening to him. I am his passage between life and death and for him to be able to recover and go back, I need to let him go... I am the reason he is still in a coma.

ALBERTO

Woa woa woa... hold on one second there, Amy. Don't give your- self so much credit. He clearly has a purpose with you... but, maybe you have something to teach him too.

AMY
What could I possibly teach him?

ALBERTO
I think it's more of "what can you help him with... or his family?

AMY
Just promise me you'll never leave.

ALBERTO
I can't, I'm leaving in three weeks remember. Blame that on the calendar.

AMY
I mean from my life, moron. Promise me we'll be friends forever.

ALBERTO
I promise.

AMY
I love you.

ALBERTO
I love you too, boo.

Without a doubt he gave me peace, and I needed it. He stood next to me until I fell asleep. I woke up the next morning and he wasn't there anymore.

FOREVER VS. NEVER

"Involved in the promises we make, but never keep, The ones that time always denies; the verbal conjugations we should never pronounce, But that we always use to make empty promises".

FRIENDS FOREVER

By 'friend' we understand that we talk about the one person who is always present during difficult times and doesn't walk away.

Or he shouldn't, but I think a true friend goes beyond that. A friend is one who makes mistakes, the one who forgives and stays regardless...

A friend who pushes you to do things that you are afraid of or that make you feel insecure, and that you often end up thanking them for challenging you to do it, because it made you a better person and because thanks to that "advice" you grew up, it helped you achieve something in your career and expose you to an unknown world, and without a doubt: made you happy.

A friend shows you the way to make the impossible, possible.

But a friend is also one who might be absent sometimes, maybe they can't be there in a way, but one way or another, they always come back.

They can't always support you during the bad moments, and out of love they decide to step back, because sometimes we just don't have enough positive energy to share and it's better to back off to not affect others with our bad vibes or problems.

Sometimes it's better to say:
Hey, I can't right now, I don't even have the strength to care for myself" instead of pretending to hear or care for your problems without actually listening; it's better than to be mentally absent, but physically present, that is part of being honest.

We are all human and absence doesn't define us: It's the courage we have to express our feelings, even if they involve being selfish for a minute, that is what really defines us.

There are friends for beers and parties, others to have long talks with a glass of wine.

Or to cry and celebrate achievements, also those who become your family even though you don't have the same bloodline.

Those who balance your days when you can't even think, and some others with whom you watch the world cup or go to the movies.

There are so many types of friends, some that are for everything, even when they can't be and rather be nothing, because they know that deep down when the time is right, you will understand their motives and forgive their absence.

Life goes on, and if it's real you'll find your way back to each other, without minding the circumstances.

A friend means forever, and I speak for myself when I profoundly thank the Universe for always giving me real friends.

I won't lie, some have left, but not without leaving an important lesson in my life, they were good friends while it lasted.

Others, the most important ones, got to my life to stay forever and trust me, if you leave... I'll leave right behind you.

To me, the word 'friend' is a human being or unknown species whom I wouldn't be able to live without...
You can get over one night stands, a street love, a long lasting relationship, but a good friendship? Those with whom you

laugh, cry, feel their pain and they feel yours.
The one who pay for your drinks even when they can't even pay for their own.

Those you never forget, those you never get over.

There are friends for everything, and some friends are everything.

I am writing this for you, my lifetime friends and also to those I just met, because time does not define the strength of the now: it's more likely that the now defines the time it will last forever even after those memories are forgotten by the death of our bodies.

Remember something:

We can't be friends with everybody. The fact that sometimes I was not a good friend to someone, doesn't make me a bad friend. It's just that you can't be a friend to everyone, because we were not all born to connect, we were born to understand that each of us have a path to follow and those who are destined to be part of the path, stay with us, and those who are not, they are just a brief lessons that will be driven apart when the time is right.

"It's the audacity, the trust and the bravery to let yourself be seen vulnerable by those we believe are our friends that builds a strong friendship. "

JULY 29TH, 2008.

I got to my room after my Volleyball practice. The tournament is about to start and I am dead nervous, it will be my first time playing in a team; if I don't do it right, I will be disappointing the rest of the team, my coach, my parents and most importantly, myself. I had english class and it was okay, the bullies are not paying attention to me anymore, thank God. I have been feeling more confident and third parties don't get to me that easily.

I had an appointment with the psychologist in the afternoon, she showed me the changes I have made from when I got to the school till the present day through the game of questions we always play. I guess it's her way of stimulating and make me conscious of my feelings without thinking too much. Even when I don't even know they are there. Like fear, for example. I feel like it's constantly a part of me, but I am avoiding being aware of him, I guess because I am afraid that it will take over me. Lately I have been finding a balance between my negative emotions and my positive ones.

PSYCHOLOGIST

How are you feeling today.

AMY

At peace.

PSYCHOLOGIST

How are your activities?

AMY

Enjoyables.

PSYCHOLOGIST

Your family?

AMY

Unstable.

PSYCHOLOGIST

Alberto?

AMY

Unconditional.

PSYCHOLOGIST

Tito?

AMY

Same.

PSYCHOLOGIST

What does life mean to you?

AMY

Opportunities.

PSYCHOLOGIST

Who is the person you love the most?

AMY

My brother.

PSYCHOLOGIST

What do you think about death?

AMY

Natural.

PSYCHOLOGIST

What are your dreams?

AMY

Alternate realities.

PSYCHOLOGIST
What is your passion?

AMY
Art.

PSYCHOLOGIST
How do you feel now?

AMY
Free.

PSYCHOLOGIST
Can you feel the change? You are more positive, enthusiastic. More passionate and emotionally mature, Amy.

"Beyond understanding the meaning of evolution, the most important thing during its path: is to feel it."

I was outside Tito's house, I could see Orly from afar stepping down from the car along with Tito in her arms very smiley and energetic, she kissed him on the forehead and walked together into the house. I followed them and kept myself as close as possible, looking at them from a corner. In that moment the hologram version of Tito appeared next to me and we would look at his family and himself having dinner together, happy. It was shabbat night (from what I learned from Alberto): they had everything prepared and as always when together they were extremely united. Suddenly the scene had an unexpected turn: Tito wasn't in Orly's arms anymore, but in a wheel chair pushed by a nurse.

They walked in and Tito's hologram started blinking. They reunited in the dining room and had dinner together even though the family's energy and vibe wasn't the same they still continued with their tradition. Orly's husband took her hand and smiled at her, giving her an ethereal mo- ment of happiness for the family. Tito stopped blinking and was completely present next to me. He would pull me by my shirt to walk through a door that led us to my house where I saw my parents eating separately, in different tables, they both looked miserable and when I turned my back I saw my brother laying on his bed. He sat on the edge of the bed and started scrolling down the pictures he took of us together with his camera... I guess he misses me. I briefly smiled, and then from one second to the next both Tito and I were walking in our park.

This time, instead of walking he ran all over the place, we were running together. A part of me wanted to say goodbye, because it was time for him to go back to his family; it wasn't fair that I would keep him connected to me just to find him in my dreams. I saw Tito's family in the distance, the kids all looked older, Tito wasn't with them but they looked happy; I saw balloons attached to the table with the number 8. They all sang 'Happy Birthday' looking at the sky and blew the candle. Tito took my hand, and once again showed me my parents and my brother eating all together, yet still miserable, as if something was missing and I guess it was me. Even though we weren't happy before I left to boarding school I feel like we would compliment each other in our own way, regardless of the circumstances. Little by little I was beggining to understand Tito's purpose in my dreams, and they would fill my heart with hope, but also with fear about the possible future that awaits me.

I wanted to go back home; Alberto was almost done with the summer camp and I wanted to be with my family. Maybe I don't have the final word to fix things, but at least I could share with them the light Tito and Alberto are giving me; instead of being a burden or a tragedy, I could now be a support and a little bit more understanding with my parents, opposite from the selfish person I was before leaving.

WHAT IS VS. WHAT MEANS?

"We think we understand, but actually, we don't even have a clue".

Life is (or at least that's what I believe) what we make of it, what we learn from it and what we think we 'know' or 'understand' by the concept of "life".

But I wonder, What is life? Aside from breathing, feeling and coexisting? What the fuck is life?

I stopped asking myself that and I just started 'living', while I still question everything I see and touch, just as much as what I believe and what I don't.

I live a solivagant life.

I know none of my questions will have a "reasonable" answer, (if you know what I mean by that) Not just the basic ones, you know?

"Why did he leave me?"
"What did I do to deserve this?
"Why doesn't he love me?

Why? Why? Why?....

Over and over again, and none of them have a helpful answer, yet.

Because the answer depends on who is asking the question, and if you let an answer that was not meant for you get to you, meaning: if you take it personal, it could ruin your life.

The answer to a third party's question has nothing to do with you, just like when you are the question, the answer has nothing to do with the rest of the world.

Why is this happening to you? Or me... for the sake of saying it.

Because we allow it to happen, unconsciously, but we are the ones that give it permission to touch us and affect us.

Why?

Fuck, I don't know, it just does.

I say this just to be able to continue because I've always told myself that "just because" or "simple no" are not the right answers, but the questions of "what, how, when and where? About the universe, they don't have a truthful and reliable answer, it's always different.

Time? Space? Infinite? Eternity? Present? Future? Past? Forgiveness? Where are all of those things that life teaches us about? Do we actually see it? I don't think we can see them because it's a feeling that we keep within: we are made up of all of the questions we ask ourselves daily. We are our own answers, we are our own forgiveness to the mistakes we make... **WE ARE***, as simple as that... we are.*

Alberto finished reading the writing I showed him; it was the first time I shared something without being asked to.

ALBERTO
I love it, it's amazing. Are you thinking of sharing it or am I going to be the ghost friend that has to hide your talent?

AMY
I've been thinking about it, but I don't like the name you gave it. I am still not sure, I don't feel con- fident enough. But thinking about it is a big step, at least I shared it without you asking or sneaking into my things.

ALBERTO
I'm sorry, I am a curious human.

AMY
Gossipmonger is what you are.

ALBERTO
Somebody has to push you.

AMY
I know, your are right... but, what about you? Who pushes you?

ALBERTO
We are here for each other, aren't we?

AMY
I would love to say yes, but... I started thinking the other day and... I don't know anything about you.

ALBERTO

You know enough: I'm funny, smart, philosopher, and I make you laugh a lot.

AMY

Of course, that is who you are with me. But who are you really? What comes after your name? I don't even know your last name.

ALBERTO

Cohen.

AMY

So you are jewish!

ALBERTO

Duuhhh... Doesn't my face says it all?

AMY

Ugh, I can't with you, but okay. Don't tell me anything, either way you are leaving, so...

ALBERTO

I promised you I wouldn't.

AMY

So what are we going to do? Text everyday?

ALBERTO

(prankrish)

Or in your dreams.

AMY

I guess.

ALBERTO

Amy, there are so many ways to stay in touch, it doesn't always have to be physically.

AMY

Telepathy?

ALBERTO

Why are you acting like this?

AMY

Because you know everything about me and I don't know any- thing about you. I don't know if I'm being selfish because we are always talking about me, me, me.... Or is it because you don't trust me?

ALBERTO

We are different. I don't tend to talk about myself, nor my problems.

AMY

Why?

ALBERTO

Because I don't have problems.

AMY

What do you mean? We all have them, Alberto. For God's sake.

ALBERTO

Alah.

AMY

Don't try to be funny right now, we are fighting.

ALBERTO
(laughing)

We? That sounds like a party. You are fighting by yourself. Take a chill pill, breath, let it go. You will have to work double if you get mad.

AMY
Don't change the subject!

ALBERTO
What do you want me to say? I don't have problems. I chose to spend a happy-problemless life.

AMY
What about your family?

ALBERTO
Well, my father is very religious; I have three brothers, all older than me. My mom is the most beautiful human being I have ever met, she has a non profit foundation for low income children. And... I don't know, we are all very Jewish.

AMY
Okay, that's something. See? I know you a little bit more now.

ALBERTO
Feeling better? Spice girl.

AMY
No, because I had to ask you and basically force you to tell me.

ALBERTO

You are right, but keep in mind that you are going through a lot of changes and sometimes you just need to be heard. Besides, there is not much to tell from my side; my social life isn't very crowded, you are basically my only friend.

AMY

Why?

ALBERTO

Because I'm boring... I don't have anything to talk about and people get bored. Just like you did now.

AMY

Shut up, you are not. You are one of the most spiritual, bright guys I have ever met. Funny to its max, unconditional, smart... and you also know how to act serious sometimes.

ALBERTO

That is so true... It's so strange that people won't hang out with me, I'm great. Now that you mention it.

AMY

And an egomaniac, in case I forgot to mention it before.

Alberto cracked up laughing.

AMY

I'm sorry I got mad, and fought with you.

ALBERTO

I know, you must be exhausted: fighting on your own for no reason and then apologize for it, ugh... too much work. But it's okay, you are a girl, you have one free pass a month with all the hormones and things you go through.

AMY

HA HA! Very funny, you should do stand up.

ALBERTO

And you should open a blog, just saying.

I kept quiet because I knew he was right. He looked at me and shared a presumed look, but as always: nice. He wasn't annoy- ing at all, it was just an arrogant but supportfull attitude, full of love, and enthusiasm. I took out my diary and began to write; he was always such an inspiration to me, he makes me want to be a better person, and I wanted to write about that, about how to appreciate the opportunities life gives you to be better or let yourself get beaten up. As he once said:

"You are one decision away from being happy, being better and living beyond just breathing."

I smiled and wrote for a little bit, then we spent the whole night talking, giving each other ideas regarding our artistic goals. He was setting up a structure for his future stand up, and I was writing for my blog. I was so proud of him even though I didn't know much about him, I knew I still had a long way to go, but he also made me feel proud of myself, of what I saw of me in his eyes. I am not in love with him: I don't see him as many would think, he is a real friend.

He taught me that a friendship between a boy and a girl does genuinely exists, showed me my worth; I was in love with the friendship we shared and built up from good feelings and intentions, without any transaction or interest behind, this is a once in a lifetime type of friendship, if you are lucky enough to find it.I stayed in his apartment, by the time I wanted to go home, it was too late to be wandering alone.

A REAL NIGHTMARE

I saw myself in my room; it was late at night and I was home alone. I walked like a zombie to my parent's room and took a bottle of sleeping pills and walked back to my room. Walked into my bathroom and sat on the floor, saw myself crying non- stop, I couldn't understand why. I stood up and stared at myself in the mirror, I saw so much anger and resentfulness in my eyes, full of unanswered questions. I could see it in my reflec- tion; I took one pill from the bottle and when I was about to take it I saw a way out of this living nightmare in that bottle full of sleeping pills. I decided to take all of them. I relived that mo- ment of my life and understood what happened: I walked back to my bed and slowly fell asleep crying, clinging to my pillow. Hours went by fast and by morning my brother was knocking on my door to go to school; I walked towards the bathroom without enough strength and I saw myself holding onto the sink and fainted right away, hitting my head so strong I started bleeding. I was yelling for help, even though I knew no one could listen: I was reliving it all in a dream. My mom walked in and found me lying on the floor, she sat on her knees calling my brother desperately. I couldn't help but feel guilty; I saw my brother walking in and I saw how his jackass face changed... he was shaking nervous and for a few seconds doubted, he didn't know what to do, but one of my brother's biggest qualities is that he knows how to find solutions to problems, sometimes by ignoring them. But this time wasn't a good time to ignore the problem.

CHAPTER 6

BEFORE THE AFTERTIME..

"All this running to find myself in my nightmare called reality."

TIME TRAVEL

BACK to MAY 17tH

DEREK

(walking from side to side)

Fuck, fuck, fuck... fuck mom. Okay, relax, I am calling 911 and everthing will be okay. Stay here with Amy.

ANGELA

(shaking)

No, there is no time. Stay with her I'll go get the car.

Derek took my mother's place and held me, she ran. Derek carried me and took me to our building's entrance where my mom was waiting; she stepped down and got in the backseat with me and my brother started driving as fast as he ever did. My mom was crying and trying to dial my dad's number, but he wasn't picking up.

ANGELA

(shaking Amy)

Baby, what happened? Please talk to me. Amy, please wake up.

(shaking her stronger.)

Talk to me, Amy please.

DEREK

(holding Angela's hand)

Mom, it's okay we are almost there.

We entered the ER; Derek and my mom stood in the entrance, devastated as I was being wheeled in by the doctors. I saw myself lying on the stretchers while doctors were talking about a cardiac arrest; they were doing electroshocks over and over again, but I wouldn't come back.

I woke up crying, Alberto was next to me. I now remembered the reason why I came to a new country to 'start over'; my inner voice started talking to me, and accepted that it was all my fault. I tried to take my own life and my resentment at her, at life is that I failed. I couldn't beat destiny: that is my actual anger towards the world. But now, what truly hurts is that I lived, and Tito didn't.

When you try to defy destiny and lose against it, you live a rewarded defeat, because you get a second chance to feel and learn to live. Some won't run with the same luck, because their destiny wasn't to defy it, but to fulfill it.

Even though my mom was in denial for a long time, it was time for me to be honest. Now that I am conscious about what really happened, I needed to share it with the only person that has always believed in me.

AMY

I tried to commit suicide.

ALBERTO

What? When? Why? Amy, what are you talking about?

AMY

Relax, it was before coming here. That's the reason why I'm here.

ALBERTO

Why didn't you tell me before?

AMY

I wasn't trying to keep it from you, I didn't remember all of it. But I had a dream about it and relieved the whole thing. I am not proud of it. I know I was being a coward.

ALBERTO

(smug)

Well, you got to know me, and you would still be the same miserable person you were when I met you. The result to this cowardly act of yours, led you to meet the best thing that has ever happened to you... me.

AMY

I'm sorry I lied.

ALBERTO

You didn't lie to me. You were lying to yourself.

AMY

Ouch!

ALBERTO

I'm not trying to hurt you... it's just the truth.

AMY

I know, but one thing I noticed is that Tito wasn't in this dream with me.

ALBERTO

Because he has nothing to do with the decision you made.

AMY

Then why was he in all of the others?

ALBERTO

What happens in the other dreams?

AMY

He shows me his family and the accident, sometimes my family.

ALBERTO

He is showing you the things you refuse to see on your own. Your dreams, your reality, that is some- thing you could see for yourself but you were too afraid to face the truth. But hey, listen, don't forget that due to that tragedy, you're here. And I happened to you, so... you're welcome.

AMY

You are never going to change, right?

ALBERTO

Why would I? I'm awesome.

AMY

As long as you stay.

ALBERTO

The point is that you already know who you are, and now you can explore what's beyond yourself and make art out of your broken pieces.

AMY

And what about him?

Alberto didn't say a word, and I was just laying in his sofa. I felt so peaceful and light, for the first time I was free from my mind constantly judging me.

AUGUST 1st.

Orly was lying next to Tito in his bed while reading him a book and holding his hand softly to not mess with any of the machines and cables. He was still in a coma, but Orly was still attached to science and faith. She closed the book and as she was putting it on the shelf where a lot of other books were standing, she saw Tito's album from when he was born. She took it and sat next to him, again. Tito was by the door next to me, clinging to my leg. Orly was showing him all the pictures as if he was alive, from his birth to the last picture she took of him before the accident. All of a sudden Orly broke into tears, and closed the book when suddenly a paper fell to the floor, I could notice that it was the same drawing Tito gave me in the park, made with crayons, a very childish drawing of his family. Orly half smiled and opened the album to put back the drawing and on the page she opened it, there was his handprint. Orly lost herself in her thoughts for a few seconds.

ORLY

(joyfull)

AHA! That's it, G-d Thank you! Robertoooo. Come, hurry up. It his mark!

Roberto entered the room worried; Orly hugged him. Tito, standing next to me smiled softly and tender.

ROBERTO

What's going on?

ORLY

It's his mark, look, it's Tito's mark.

ROBERTO

I see that, but what do you mean by that?

ORLY
Look how strong he marked his handprint?

ROBERTO
I don't understand what you're trying to tell me with this.

The sound vanished and we were in a white room. I bent my knees to hug him and for the first time I could see his eyes from the same height; in that moment I understood that from my height I wasn't able to.

Now we traveled to our park. Tito was attached to so many blue balloons, of all sizes and shapes, so many that he was being lifted by them. As soon as I realized he was al- most flying I cut off all the strings so they wouldn't lift him up anymore. I wasn't able to save all of the balloons, only a few of them and gave them to him so he could keep them. It was a very strange dream, to be honest. Very dense, but meaningful and happy.

I started listening to a sound that was disturbing my dream's peace; I woke up agitated and I heard Alberto knocking on the door. I ran fast towards it.

ALBERTO
Hellooooooo, good morning in the morning. What are you doing sleeping at this time girl?

AMY
It's 7:32 AM boy, what's up?

ALBERTO
Well, it turns out that I have to leave before I was supposed to.

AMY

What does "before" mean? Meaning when?

ALBERTO

Meaning... in two hours.

AMY

What? No, no. You can't You were supposed to stay for two more weeks.

ALBERTO

You could write about this dramatic moment. "Two friends separated by time".

AMY

(sad)

I mean it, why are you leaving?

ALBERTO

Well, there has been a family thing that requires my presence.

AMY

(sarcastic)

Didn't you say you didn't have problems?

ALBERTO

Alah, you have... Wait, how is that you call Alah?

AMY

Uhm... God? Jesus Christ? What does that have to do with your problems?

ALBERTO

Let me continue... God, Amy has been hanging out with me a lot. This is so beautiful, did you listen to yourself? You speak fluid sarcasm. This was just beautiful.

(reacting to the clock)

Anyway, I came to say goodbye and give you a letter, I wanted to give it to you in person.

AMY

You'll text me, right? Or e-mail me. I don't know.

ALBERTO

Duh, I walked into your life to stay and bother you even after I die okay?

AMY

You are not allowed to die before I do, okay?

ALBERTO

Me tengo que ir.

AMY

Jesus Lord, you have been hanging out with me too much. You speak fluent Spanish.

ALBERTO

Idiot! Just a little. Text me in Spanish, so I can practice. Chop Chop, I have to go.

AMY

What's the letter for?

ALBERTO
Read it only when you feel my absolute absence. Promise.

AMY
Yeah, I promise, but...

ALBERTO
I mean it. If you read it before that I will know. Everything has its own time, okay?

AMY
All right time boy, relax. Can you please tell me what happened? Why the rush?

ALBERTO
Who said rush? Smart people don't rush.

AMY
Then why are you leaving all of a sudden?

ALBERTO
I will tell you once I'm home. It's not easy for my family to live without me, literally.

AMY
Now I'll feel what your family is feeling.

ALBERTO
Most likely, yes. It's probably really hard to live without me, damn. I couldn't imagine it. Good luck with it.

AMY

Pssst, do not even. I will be call- ing you daily to spill some tea on whatever happens in this whole. Either way I'll be back in less than a year so... it'll go by fast, I hope. We have skype and emails so, no excuse. Plus, I might go for christmas, your hannukah so... we can spend it with each other's family. No?

ALBERTO

I'll take your word for it. Now come here, I need a big hug. The bus is waiting for me to go to the airport.

We hugged tightly, and he gave me a kiss on the forehead; I couldn't help but cry.

ALBERTO

Keep on writing and send me some things, I want to read what's going on in that mind of yours.

He grabbed his bag and once he was about to exit, I couldn't keep it to myself.

AMY

I'm going to miss you.

ALBERTO

(bragging)

I know.

(nostalgic)

I hope you know I will miss you too.

For the way he looked at me I knew that something happened. I have seen those eyes before and that reflection but, I couldn't remember when or where. Alberto was a happy person, all the time, 24 hours a day, and watching him like this was weird; however I respected his silence, just as he respected mine until I was ready to talk. Alberto left and a part of me left with him. I went back to sleep to forget my feelings and avoid facing the fact that I was back to being alone.

I turned to my table and Tito's drawing from my dream was in my night stand. Everything was so confusing, but with every- thing that was going on I just put the drawing in my drawer inside my diary, without giving it too much thought.

DECEMBER 3RD

I lost myself again, I have been moody the past 10 days and I don't know why. I guess it's because its been over a month since Alberto left and I haven't been able to get in touch with him, I've been sending him emails, text messages but I haven't heard from him. I feel so lonely, even though he accompanies my memories.

On the other hand, I have been having more communication with my brother: he has a girlfriend now and he is happy. Apparently my parents are still living apart, and they are about to sign the divorce papers. It makes me really sad, but deep down in my heart I had a little bit of hope that they would go back to each other.

I've also been feeling more empathetic with my mom, we are talking often; I've seen her more serene and drinking less. Classes already started and they suck. My classmates, my teachers, everything sucks, specially Alberto's absence. I haven't opened his letter because in a few days I am going back home to visit my family and I have hope that I will be able to see him like we said: for christmas and Hanukkah.

UGH, THERAPY AGAIN

PSYCHOLOGIST
You don't look well. How are you feeling?

AMY
Well in the question lies the answer: Not well.

PSYCHOLOGIST
Why?

AMY
I want to leave, I hate this place.
I'm sick of it.

PSYCHOLOGIST
Ever since you friend left you have been edgy. Your mood changed.

AMY
He was the only thing that made
my stay here, bearable.

PSYCHOLOGIST
You are still codependent, that's what we should be working on.

AMY
Why?

PSYCHOLOGIST
You still rely on someone to be happy, and you need to learn how to be happy on your own.

AMY

I am happy with myself, I just miss my family and my friend. Am I not allowed to do that?

PSYCHOLOGIST

You are not lonely enough to be accompanied. You need to learn to love the only thing that is there for you always: solitude.

TIME

I am mad at you, dear time.

Your sudden ways of taking the things we love away from us, Just to teach us that we live in a borrowed body within an illu- sion of an instant that ends even before it begins.

It hurts, and you do it to make us understand that it's up to us to be happy or to play the victim.

My advice to you, who read me:

Don't judge yourself the day you decide to play the victim; we all do at some point, and there is nothing wrong with it... it's relative, and nobody has the right to point their fingers at you for the decisions you make, because they are yours, and you are the only one capable of feeling and judging your own life: it's yours and only yours.

At the end of the day, nobody learns from other people's experiences, and being unconditional doesn't mean you won't be judged by those who love you: it just means they will be there regardless... It doesn't matter if they judge you or question your decisions. They stay with you and that's what truly matters.

Some people come and take the human body to accomplish a specific mission; and then leave. Or that's how we feel when their bodies leave, when we don't have the chance to hug them again.

As a reaction we are filled with anger, madness and ego, and here I am judging time and blaming him for taking the one thing that made me feel better. But the reality is that everything works under its own clock, missions and moments. It has nothing to do with us or our feelings.

Everything happens in a brief instant in which your eyes are closed and through a sigh you realize that there is a universe within yourself... and I saw that universe in my dreams. Time, please... don't take that universe away from me.

DECEMBER 18tH

The most anticipated day of the year arrived. I was going back home, even though it was only for two weeks I was very excited. I was ready to feel the home vibe after being away for a while.

My brother and my parents were there to receive me at the airport. We immersed ourselves in a family hug I have never felt before. I learned that sometimes we need to spend some time apart to value each other's company and build a stronger bond. I asked myself if that would work with my parents... but it was a stupid question, I was in the car heading to a new reality: at leas for me. Going home to where only my mom and brother lived, my dad... who knows where he would go.

ANGELA

Kids, what do you think about spening christmas with me and new years eve with your mom?

AMY

Can I invite a friend?

ANGELA

Alberto?

AMY

Yup.

ANGELA

Of course, I want to meet him. I don't even know what he looks like.

DEREK

(excited)

I will bring Victoria

GATE 2

AMY

Who's that?

DEREK

I told you, my girlfriend.

AMY

Oh, my bad...

DEREK

Stop it, you're gonna love her.

I was happy to spend time with them, the four of us even though I knew we were going to take separate ways again. It was hard to enter my room. I unpacked my things and lied in my bed; everything was just flashing in my mind, all the mem- ories, the hard times, this year has been tough on me but I've grown a little, now I see things from another perspective that I probably wouldn't have been able to see if I had stayed here. However, I want to come back to you, that pigsty place full of bullies and wannabes is not really my place to be. I want a new school, new friends, new environment, but what I want the most is to be with my family.

AMY

Mom! I wanted to talk to you.

ANGELA

Sure baby, tell me.

AMY

I want to start over.

ANGELA

I don't understand.

AMY

I want to come back, and stay for

good, start a new school year here... with you.

ANGELA

I don't know, Amy. Things are still frisky around here and I don't want you to be exposed or affected.

AMY

I understand, but I am already exposed to feel your absence in that place, and it gets to me. I was okay these couple of months because I had Alberto, but he left and I don't like that place. Kids are meaner than they are here.

ANGELA

Let's talk to your father about this, okay? And we'll see.

My mom looked at me with kindness and hugged me; deep down I could feel that she wanted me to stay too, but it was up to me to prove to them that I was able to do things right by staying here. I was willing to really start over: I already felt like a new me, better, but I didn't want to go back to a place that gave me no reason to be happy.

I'M SORRY, MOM.

For all the times I yelled at you, and underestimated you, blamed you for all my doubts.

Sorry that I didn't tell you this before, but I felt like I was drowning, I felt despised by you, and seeing you like that: amongst tears and alcohol, diving in music, broke me little by little.

You were living in your own world, far away from mine.

I felt I didn't fit in yours.

Just as I felt like you didn't fit in my own.

Now I understand that the world isn't world without you, just an empty circle, without purpose.

Without you, everything turns into nothing, now I get it, you are everything.

I'm sorry for the times I made you cry, with the excuse that I was hurt by you.

For all the times I gave you a motive
to doubt your abilities as a mom.

Thank you for never leaving me, even though I was mean, for staying and supporting my wishes, for hugging me when I didn't want to, but needed it.

for missing me when I was gone, for letting me fly away, even if that meant walking away from you.

For all the times I've had to run away, the struggles to accomplish my dreams, even if they are not what you planned for me, for respecting my goals, for letting me be a walking dreamer.

I'm sorry, mom.

Because now I get it, a mother shouldn't be judged or pointed at, a mother should not be conditioned, nor sanctioned, mother means forever.

Forever means you.

I LOVE YOU MOM.

I, AM SORRY, DAD.

For all the times I judged your decisions, for not being what you dreamed your daughter to be, for not understanding your behavior.

I am sorry for not apologizing before, for not regretting my mistakes, because even though I hurt you, I can't regret the things that made me who I am today.

I love this version of me, even though I had to beat death to reach this.

I'm done apologizing, dad.

I am actually beyond thankful, and you need to know that, because just like mom, you have always been there.

For supporting my crazy dreams, even when you didn't believe in them, for not giving up on me, even when I was about to step out.

For working so hard to afford everything me and my brother asked you for.

The education you couldn't have, but you worked to give it to us.

For pleasing my childish cravings, for the times you've cried without shame while seeing me play my music, because even though my dreams are not similar to yours, you have supported me in silence.

Without saying anything, but deep down proud as fuck.

Thank you dad, because when I thought I had nothing, I realized with you, I have everything.

I LOVE YOU ALWAYS.

CHAPTER 7

HE SAVED ME, AGAIN.

YEARS LATER...

Years went by and I never heard from Alberto again. I would write via email once a week to update him on everything that was going on in both my dreams and my daily reality. Tito's dreams weren't as constant as they used to be; I supposed I was letting him go little by little, but either way every time he visited me in my dreams it was lovely and fun, special and truly present. I even got to talk to him about Alberto; clearly there wasn't much Tito would say, he was a three year old, but he would listen and he even made a drawing of us once, and through his silence I would find answers every now and then.

I always had Alberto's letter in my drawer, but a part of me always felt him very close even though I was mad at him, I never wanted to open it; I guess I was afraid of what it would say. I mean, what type of friend leaves promising to always be there for you and then disappear? I didn't understand anything and I was afraid to finally understand, that's why I decided to just leave it there.

On the other hand, I convinced my parents and I started over in a new school, made some great and real friends there. I fell in love a couple of times and I had a pretty good social life. Can't complain, it allowed me to actually be a joyful teenager. I graduated and by decision I moved to another state to go to college. I finished my teenage years in a healthy environment and after three years apart, my parents got back together. They're still a pretty dysfunctional couple, but deep down they're happy and I got to know what love is "regardless of..."

It was tough, I won't lie. I had a lot of happy moments, but Alberto's memory was always present and I couldn't avoid missing him all the time. Wondering what my friends and family would think of him. He was great and I really wanted him to be a part of my life forever. His essence in my life was one of the most important parts of my growth; even though he wasn't with me anymore, he left a strong mark on me.

I continued writing about my experiences and emotions, but I never opened the blog.

My dreams with Tito would summarize to a repeated image of him attached to a lot of balloons and I would cut the strings over and over again.

SEPTEMBER, 2011

I was starting my first year in college and I met a girl from my class, she was from San Francisco too. We had lunch one day, and got to know each other in the first couple of weeks. I once took my wallet out and I had Tito's picture in it, I went to buy some bottles of water for us and when I opened the wallet she saw the picture and immediately reacted to it.

— I know him, he is Tito — she said, confused and I could see the big question mark in her eyes
— from where? — I asked
— I went to high school with his older sister — she said
— Are you Jewish too? What's your last name? I asked, hoping that she would tell me more about Tito and Alberto.
— Daniela Cohen — she said.
My eyes shined, I knew it was my chance to ask her about Alberto, they had the same last time, it was obvious, I thought.

AMY
So, you know what happened to him?

DANIELA
Yes, it's a really sad story, honestly. He had an accident in his pool and drowned, the doctors resuscitated him but he is still in a coma.

AMY
What? After all these years? How? It's been too long.

DANIELA

I know, they have done all sorts of treatments, but he doesn't respond to any of them.

AMY

I see, I didn't think that... wao... Sorry you said your last name was Cohen, right?

DANIELA

Yeah.

AMY

Do you know any Alberto Cohen, by any chance?

DANIELA

I know a lot of them. The little boy, Tito, his full name is Alberto Cohen, but we are not family.

AMY

Oh... wao.

DANIELA

Where do you know him from?

AMY

We met at a summer camp in Mexico. He went back to San Francisco and I stayed there for a few more months.

DANIELA

I meant Tito.

AMY

Oh, sorry. It's a very long story but to be brief. I was at the hospital right after the accident, and I met his mom there.

I wasn't ready to talk about what really happened, much less with someone I just met; after telling Alberto, I never spoke to anyone about it again. I had it for myself, I accepted it but it was my secret. I didn't think it was necessary to be talking about it out loud. After that day I never dreamt about Tito again. I prayed for him and his family every night, wishing to the shooting starts for his recovery; and even though I always thought my dreams had some reality in them, I always had a little bit of doubt that it all might be nothing but fiction, until Daniela told me about it; and learning that my dreams were real hurt me so much, even though they were surreal interactions, there were real enough for me. Clearly we had a once in a lifetime connection.

That same year I decided to go back home and visit my family. I had a three week vacation at school and I wanted to go home for the holidays; we spent a great time together.

be safe, wherever you go,
be safe

DECEMBER 31st 2011.

I could see Tito in the distance, on a special wheelchair with a lot of machines around him and both Orly and Roberto were standing next to him. I was walking through the house on my own for some reason I was at peace, for the first time. It's hard to explain, despise of Tito's condition, there was something around that house that felt peaceful. He looked older, to be honest, but it makes sense.

It's been a few years already. All of a sudden the flat line of the heartbeat machine appeared once again, non stop; his family was around him, crying but not desperate, they had some sort of calm within their soul, as if they knew this was the moment to let go. They would just stare at him and taking his hand, loving one another. Tito appeared next to me, older, taller and more mature, but still his essence was the same, the same tender vibe.

TITO

Come.

AMY

You've grown.

TITO

Come with me.

We walked towards the door and there was our park. He was no longer next to me but holding Orly's hand in the distance, with the sunset behind. This time Orly was holding the blue balloon. Tito turned to look at me and waved his hand saying goodbye.

I woke up crying. My mom heard me and entered the room.

ANGELA

Sweetie, what's wrong?

AMY

He's gone, mom.

ANGELA

Who? What are you talking about? It was just a nightmare.

AMY

Tito.

ANGELA

Who is Tito?

AMY

The baby from the hospital.

My mom hugged me tight and laid next to me all night, consoling me since I wouldn't stop crying.

The morning after, I decided to go to the park; I wrote a letter and attached it to a blue balloon similar to the one in my dreams. As I was about to let go of everything I had to say about Tito, I heard children laughing, and I walked towards it to see who it was; and there they were, just like in my dream: Tito holding Orly's hand with the balloon. I sighed closing my eyes and the moment I opened them, Alberto was next to me. I couldn't react to his sudden presence, I was lost looking at the both of them, asking myself over and over again if I was dreaming, or living.

AMY

You think she can let him go?

ALBERTO

And you?

AMY

What about me?

ALBERTO

Can you let me go?

AMY

You already left.

ALBERTO

I didn't and you know it.

AMY

(confused)

Where the fuck are you then?

ALBERTO

If I had left, you would have opened the letter.

I woke up, it was clearly a dream; or an alternate reality, I no longer know anymore. I couldn't help but smile along with some tears falling down my cheeks. I ran to my desk and took Alberto's letter out, when I opened the envelope Tito's childish drawing of his family was there, the one he gave me in my dreams. The difference is that this one had *ALBERTO* as a signature, and not Tito's.

ME
DAD
Mom
BRO
Sis 1
Sis 2
Alberto

USED TO IT

by Daniel Sobrino, Dani Blau & Itai Schwartz

Maybe we should talk
lay all of our thoughts
right here on the floor

Don't want this to fade
I just wanna stay
even if we're falling apart

Running out of time you know
I don't wanna let it go
I just wanna heal you

Running out of time for us
losing moments in the dust
I just wanna hear you...

You used to hold me in the dark
right beside your open heart
I got used to it
I got used to it

You used to light me up at night
and before you said goodbye
I got used to it
I got used to it
you got me used to it
I got used to it
you got me used to it....

The ceiling's feeling short
my future is so unsure
since you cast a cloud on me

I've been feeling sore
Can't take it anymore
It feels like I am drowning in the sea

Running out of time you know
I don't wanna let it go
I just wanna heal you

Running out of time for us
losing moments in the dust
I just wanna hear you

You used to hold me in the dark
right beside your open heart
I got used to it
I got used to it

You used to light me up at night
and before you said goodbye
I got used to it
I got used to it
you got me used to it
I got used to it
you got me used to it....

Everything was foggy. And I started remembering everything I went through with Alberto, all the happy memories, the sad ones, and the thousands of dreams I had with Tito.

ALBERTO

Amy, remember... you have to look beyond what meets the eye: life is so much more than just breathing.

AMY

(desperate crying)

I don't understand.

ALBERTO

Don't resist it, don't deny your feelings and your knowledge. Here I am, I never left.

I looked through my camera roll, I was scrolling to see the pictures I had with Alberto but he wasn't in any of them. I finally went back to the park and I saw Orly, alone, with the blue balloon. Tito wasn't there and Alberto wasn't with me either.

AMY

(whispering)

Wao

I closed my eyes and a tear fell down my face; I felt how Tito and Alberto were the same person, same kindness, same eyes, same names, I understand how they were communicating with me in their own way.

ALBERTO Y TITO

Now you get it.

AMY

(immersed in tears and after sighing)

Aha...

T-Mobile LTE
11:28 AM
5%
06/23/08
5:45 PM
Edit

CHAPTER 8

AHA

NOW I GEt it

I got to an understanding that we all have a mission in life, That we choose our own reality.

I got to understand that many of us breath, but barely live, And some of us live, but barely breathe.

I understood that every person that lands in our lives Come to teach us unimaginable lessons.

I understood that the body leaves, it's borrowed and when the time comes, it vanishes, because the connections between two souls destined to remain together, are marked by an amazing 'forevers' that a physical life can't continue, we believe we disappear, but that's not true. I recognized him.

I understood that Tito came into my life in an innocent form, to help me live, and me, that simple teenage girl I was 5 years ago got to Tito's life to walk through earth and help him leave his mark, the one he left in me, and wake up those who walk but are dead inside.

I understood that Alberto came into my life to help me see what my adolescent mind wouldn't allow me to see within Tito's innocence.

I got that his innocence and random occurrences were just clues to help me discover my own path.

I got that it wasn't about starting over, but continuing by accepting and respecting my past, loving and creating my presente, to be able to deserve my future.

I understood that earthly time and the word "forever" are ethereal, but it actually started to never end that day I met him in my dreams, at the hospital.

I understood his mission and mine, and that's why im here telling you what I wasn't brave enough to tell you, because I was afraid people would judge me.

I got that we all make mistakes, and that is part of existing.

I understood that, yes I might have gone through shitty moments in my adolescence, and many of you might not understand them, but life gave me the most wonderful gift.

An amazing 'forever' that I will never forget, and the mistakes I made, that came with the lessons I now practice.

Life gifted me with real friends, and the best of the best best friend, with the most amazing dysfunctional family ever..

It gave my a baby that gave me back my life, even when that meant leaving his.

All those shitty moments were all worthy to remind me of who I am today, the reason why I exist, because I also understood that you do nothing with knowing, if you're not doing anything about it.

Life gave me my AHA moment after suppressing it for so long: I took action and started living, I opened my eyes and did something with the things I now know.

Life gifted me with life itself, and it doesn't matter what comes next, the after joy will always be worth it.

Friedich Nietzsche once said:

"He who has a why to live can bear almost any how."

MORE THAN LIVING, I'M ALIVE

I am still the same Amy I was back in the day, but I realized I'm extraordinary and my superpower is the ability to dream... and I'm not talking about goals, I'm talking about the dreams that led me to him, to meet him, lucid and real that guided me to feel like I was born again.

"Breathing isn't a sign of life, but feeling. Because dying is the only thing that lets us know that we lived."

Nowadays I know that school is just a phase in life, that bullying comes from within the moment we don't stand up for ourselves, that problems come and go.

That we all have a mission in this life, and all the afterlives, and not even by being owners of our own life we have the right to decide when to end it. We belong to destiny, and no matter the circumstances we have to respect the beautiful illusion time is and let the moment be, good or bad, they always end, and there has always been the answer to any WHY's we might have.

It doesn't matter how long or short our path is through this planet, it's about how strong we walk to leave our print. I know it's hard to understand, I wanted to leave before my time was over, because I was being pressured by sosciety to be what they wanted me to be, I wanted to run away from my family's problems instead of trying to be the light that shines amongst us and heal them.

I wanted to run away and I was selfish, I know that. It is part of life and it might sound awful but I don't regret it, not even a second of it, because thanks to that, I met the light of my life. Thanks to those moments of questions, doubts, and wildness I let myself be discovered by my destiny and throw myself to death that led me, instead, to a path where I felt I was born again, a spiritual path that made me who I am.

My angels made me understand that time is just an illusion and that we dream about a reality while we live in the wrong life, there is always a hidden message behind every thought, every dream, every action, every intention.

We are part of the message we came to say out loud, to pass to others. We might not change the world, but we might change someone else's world and make it better.

MAYBE

Maybe if you, bullied students, raise your voice: you might inspire others that are going through the same thing you are going through to make them stronger and stand up for themselves, to understand that this is just a phase and that at some point, it will be over.

Maybe if you, mother or father are going through a hard patch in your marriage, or with your kids, you should raise your voice and focus on finding solutions instead of drowning in the problem.

Maybe if you, beautiful human who feels abandoned by your brother or sister, or even your parents, If you feel lonely, you could raise your voice and maybe, be the one who changes the dynamic and bring them together.

Maybe if you speak your pain, mother that is mourning the loss of a child, you could be someone else's resilience.

Raise your voice, person who has doubts regarding what life is about, and why the pain and tragedies are so necessary, you could ask others and realize that you are not alone, that a lot of people are also asking themselves why this happened to them.

Raise your voice, you beautiful human being doubting of your extraordinary abilities. Pick up those broken pieces and make art with them. You will change someone's life and you might not even know it, but someday you will understand that you have accomplished your mission and will be able to leave in peace, without doubting, without even looking for it, without rushing it... you would have lived a happy and beautiful life.

I don't know you, but I already love you. I raise my writing in the name of my voice, I told you my story and I hope one day you could look at yourself in the mirror and smile at how bright and beautiful you are both inside and out, because that will be the reason of who you will become tomorrow, and I am sure you will shine so bright that you will be thankful for all the “why’s” life puts you through.

SPECiAL tHANKS

Maria Aristeiguieta, Carlos Perez, Andres Perez & Victoria Muller.

Miriam Aristeiguieta, Luis Aristeiguieta & Irene Aristeiguieta.

Fernando Perez, Mariano Perez, Rafael Perez, Mercedes Perez & Horacio Perez.

Jose E. Tinoco, Maria E Benitez, Oriana Tinoco, Maria C Benitez & Luis D. Aristeiguieta.

Alma Matrecito, Angela Rincon, Carmen de Leon, Jessymar Urdaneta, Ana Lorena Sanchez, Triana García, Laura Chimaras & Melissa Carvajal.

Emilia Tosta, Emily Tosta, Gabriela Tosta & Karla Tosta.

Joel Seidl, Kevin Cohen, Daniel Sobrino, Carlos Arrechea, Daniel Demenezes, Alejandro Sequera, Riccardo Frascari, Salomon Benacerraf, Manuel Ujueta, Jose Feng, Abiram Brizuela, Alberto Arvelo, Jorchual Vargas, Thiago Muller & Burno Romano.

Alana Marshall, Sofía García, Leopoldo Van den Brande & August Isern.

YOU ARE SOMEONE ELSE'S VOICE, BUT WHEN YOU CAN'T EVEN LISTEN TO YOURSELF, SPEAK A LITTLE LOUDER. THERE YOU ARE, AND YOU WILL SEE YOURSELF.

In honor of
Alberto Moises Cohen Meir
(June 20, 2006 - January 31st, 2012)

If you want to contribute to

'dejando mi huella' non profit

please contact:

fundaciondejandomihuella.com

Made in the USA
Middletown, DE
15 February 2022

61113583R00118